# The Lighthouse

*The Aegis Netowrk*

## The Sarich Brothers Series
Book 1

## Jen Talty

# Praise for Jen Talty

"I positively loved *In Two Weeks*, and highly recommend it. The writing is wonderful, the story is fantastic, and the characters will keep you coming back for more. I can't wait to get my hands on future installments of the NYS Troopers series." *Long and Short Reviews*

"*In Two Weeks* hooks the reader from page one. This is a fast paced story where the development of the romance grabs you emotionally and the suspense keeps you sitting on the edge of your chair. Great characters, great writing, and a believable plot that can be a warning to all of us." *Desiree Holt, USA Today Bestseller*

"*Dark Water* delivers an engaging portrait of wounded hearts as the memorable characters take you on a healing journey of love. A mysterious death brings danger and intrigue into the drama, while sultry passions brew into a believable plot that melts the reader's heart. Jen Talty pens an entertaining romance that grips the heart as the colorful and dangerous story unfolds into a chilling ending." *Night Owl Reviews*

"This is not the typical love story, nor is it the typical mystery. The characters are well rounded and interesting." *You Gotta Read Reviews*

"*Deadly Secrets* is the best of romance and suspense in one hot read!" *NYT Bestselling Author Jennifer Probst*

"A charming setting and a steamy couple heat up the pages in an suspenseful story I couldn't put down!" *NY Times and USA today Bestselling Author Donna Grant*

"*Murder in Paradise Bay* is a fast-paced romantic thriller with plenty of twists and turns to keep you guessing until the end. You won't want to miss this one..." *USA Today bestselling author Janice Maynard*

*To past friends for showing me the way and teaching me the value of what real friendship means.*

*A special thank you to LISA HEMMING. Your support humbles me. Thank you.*

# A Note From Jen Talty

Some researchers have said there is a correlation between the ocean and being calm, happier, and more creative. Having spent a winter in Jupiter, Florida, I'd say these researchers are right on the money.

The SARICH BROTHERS series was born while I spent four months in Jupiter, walking the beach, visiting the Jupiter Lighthouse, driving around Jupiter Island, dining at various places on the water, and overall enjoying this next chapter in my life known as the 'empty nest.'

The Sarich brothers, while poor, had a good life, raised by loving parents. However, their father was killed in the line of duty when the oldest boy was just twenty and the youngest fourteen, changing their lives forever...

Each of the brothers struggle with a restlessness, in part caused by their father's death. They are strong, honorable, and loyal men. They aren't looking for a woman, as their jobs aren't necessarily conducive with long-term relationships. It's going to take an equally strong woman to rip down the Sarich brothers' defenses and help them settle their restlessness, so they can give their hearts.

The series does not need to be read in order, but the four novellas do follow a timeline.

Come join each of the Sarich boys in their journey to heal old wounds, mend broken hearts, and find their way to true happiness with the love of a good, strong woman.

And I'd love for you to checkout the spin-off series:

## THE AEGIS NETWORK: THE EVERGLADES DIVISION

In a place where the past never stays buried and the swamp keeps its own score, they're not just protecting the land—they're fighting to reclaim it.

**Starting with the first two books:**

*Hunted in Calusa Cove*

*Shadows in Calusa Cove*

Grab a glass of vino, kick back, relax, and let the romance roll in...

Sign up for my _Newsletter_ _(https://dl.bookfunnel._ _com/82gm8b9k4y.)_ where I often give away free books before publication.

Join my private Facebook group (https://www. facebook.com/groups/191706547909047/) where I post exclusive excerpts and discuss all things murder and love!

# Welcome to THE AEGIS NETWORK

The Aegis Network is the brainchild of former Marines, Bain Asher and Decker Griggs. While serving their country, Bain and Decker were injured in a raid in an undisclosed area during an unsanctioned mission. Instead of twiddling their thumbs while on medical leave, they focused their frustration at being sidelined toward their pet project: a sophisticated Quantum Communication Network Satellite. When the devastating news came that neither man would be placed on active duty ever again, they sold their technology to the United States government and landed on a heaping pot of gold and funded their passion.

Saving lives.

The Aegis Network is an elite group of men and women, mostly ex-military, descending from all branches. They may have left the armed forces, but the armed forces didn't leave them. There's no limit to the type of missions they'll take, from kidnapping, protection detail, infiltrating enemy lines, and everything in between; no job is too big or too small when lives are at stake.

As Marines, they vowed no man left behind. As civilians, they will risk all to ensure the safety of their clients.

# Chapter One

Logan Sarich dumped his rucksack in the lobby of The Aegis Network main building, well aware he hadn't showered in forty-eight hours and the Orlando summer humidity clung to his pores like flies on shit. "Hey, Ashley." He leaned against her desk and smiled. Normally, he'd go clean up after an op, but Ashley's message said it was urgent. "Where's Asher and Decker?" He bit back a chuckle. He always wanted to say black n' decker when discussing his bosses and the co-founders of The Aegis Network.

"Talking with a client," Ashley said, plugging her nose. "What's that smell?"

"A combination of two days of surveillance, stale

coffee, fish tacos, a hot dog, and something I can't pronounce," Logan said, smiling. "You told me, and I quote, to get my ass to the office."

She shook her head. "No, I said to get your cute little tush in here as soon as you can. Next time wash that ripe smell off before you enter my space."

"Yes, ma'am." Logan had only been working for The Aegis Network for six months, after spending six years in the Special Forces, and before that, six years in the infantry. "I can leave and come back, if you'd prefer."

"I've smelled worse." She pushed a file toward the end of the table. "You've been assigned a new case."

He'd been hoping for a couple of days off, but he'd taken this job under the premise that all he wanted to do was work.

Be careful what you ask for.

He picked up the file.

"In Jupiter, Florida," she said.

He didn't open the file, just peered over the top. "The bosses want me to go to my hometown for a job?"

"Open it." Ashley crossed her legs, swiveling the chair.

Logan did as asked but frowned the moment he

saw a picture of Mia Vanderlin and her twin brother Markus. "My mother works for the Vanderlins. I can't take this job."

"I was told you'd say that." Ashley waggled her brow. "And I was told to inform you that you have no choice. You know the layout, the people, so you're the best man for the job."

Logan had learned his first week on the job not to argue with Ashley. She might not be the boss, but she ran this place for the bosses, and she was a force to be reckoned with. "What's the assignment?"

"Bodyguard."

"Of the twins?" He flipped through the pages, ignoring the childhood memories of skinny-dipping with the smartest and sexiest girl in school. "Why?"

"Mia and Markus are ethical hackers. Mia was hired to do a security check for DANA Corp."

"The defense contractor?"

Ashley nodded. "While doing the check, Mia found some sort of virus that swapped out good specs with bad ones."

"So, stealing information from DANA Corp?"

"Decker believes an organization known as STEALTH was behind the attack, but it hasn't been confirmed."

"I take it she blew the whistle?"

"Not at first."

"Please don't tell me she messed with the a-holes in STEALTH." But Logan knew the answer. When messed with, Mia tended to fight back.

"She created a program that would spit out false information to STEALTH regarding various defense contracts and designs on some top-secret material. She also managed to send a message to the CIA, who were able to trace the origin of the original hack back to an abandoned warehouse. The CIA have people in custody. None of them are talking."

"Where?"

"Like the CIA is going to tell us that." She held her hand up. "Not that Asher and Decker didn't try, so let's focus on the assignment."

Logan still knew a few people at the Agency, and he suspected his boss knew that he'd use his contacts. "If she's the one who ratted out STEALTH, why does Markus need protection?"

"STEALTH threatened Mia directly, but since they are business partners, she thinks he could be a target as well."

Logan should dump the file back on Ashley's desk and inform his bosses this was one job he'd have to say no to. While it would be good to see Mia and her brother again, no way would he be setting foot on that property. "Why isn't the CIA protecting them?"

"They have bigger issues to deal with, like a breach in security, so when Mia was threatened, her family called us."

"We are the best." Logan tried not to wince at the memory of the last time he'd been at Mia's house. "I'm grateful for the work, but seriously, someone else has to take this one, and I'll need your help to convince the bosses. I know for a fact that Mr. and Mrs. Vanderlin will take one look at me and slam the door in my face."

"Dressed like that." She pointed at his muddy T-shirt that used to be white. "And smelling like a cow pasture, I'm sure they would, but I'm guessing that's not why you want to go running for the hills."

"My skill set is better suited for other ops. I'm not cut out to be a babysitter for a bunch of rich people."

"Asher and Decker won't see that as a good reason to reassign." She leaned back in her chair, crossing her arms, almost daring him to continue arguing with her.

"There might be a little bad history there," Logan admitted.

"Such as?"

The corners of his mouth tugged upward into a smile. The incident had been both part of the best times of his life, and the most embarrassing. "The Vanderlins think I deflowered Mia."

"Deflowered? Really?" Ashley laughed, tossing her long hair behind her shoulder. "I never thought a word like that would come out of your mouth," she said.

"It's the word they used when they told my mother they caught me in Mia's bedroom with my pants down."

"So, it's true?" Ashley cocked her head, her face turned serious.

"Let's just say we deflowered each other." He covered his mouth, gliding his hand down to his chin, trying to wipe off the grin. There hasn't been a time in his adult life where remembering Mia didn't make him smile. He often wondered if she thought of him the same way.

"Well, it was the family who requested you personally, so I think you're screwed."

"Yes, ma'am." He picked up his rucksack, flinging it over his shoulder. "When?"

"Right after you shower. It's only a two-hour drive."

"I've done it in less," he said as he turned toward the door.

"And Logan," Ashley said, her words laced with humor. "Don't sleep with the client."

# Chapter Two

Mia stepped onto the second-story patio and inhaled sharply, letting the salty breeze fill her lungs as she watched the ocean waves crash against the beach on Jupiter Island. While she had a nice little condo overlooking the Intracoastal with a perfect view of the Jupiter Lighthouse a few miles away, nothing beat the view of the ocean from her childhood bedroom.

A few cars slowly made their way down the main road between the house and the beach. One in particular had two couples inside, and they stopped in front of the driveway, pointing, before continuing down the street. The familiar pang of loneliness still filled her mind and soul. Growing up was tough enough, but when you lived in a forty-million-dollar home *and* were the smartest girl in a public school, real friends were hard to come by.

She leaned against the railing on the patio, looking down at the gardener and his crew of seven tending to the extensive landscaping.

A black Jeep with the top off rolled to a stop in front of the gate. She lowered her sunglasses, peering over the rims, checking out the driver. His face had been blocked by the sunrays reflecting off the front windshield. His bulky arm reached over the truck door, hitting the intercom. The buzzing of a weed trimmer covered the sound of his voice.

The front gates swung open, and the Jeep pulled around the circular driveway, stopping just below her patio. A man with a white T-shirt eased from the front seat, his back toward her. His broad shoulders flexed as he slammed the door and reached in the back seat before turning around, looking in her direction.

She tore off her sunglasses, blinking her eyes, wondering if someone had slipped something in her smoothie this morning because no way could she be staring at Logan Sarich.

"Hey, Mia," he said, grinning. "Long time no see." He tucked his sunglasses on the collar of his shirt while holding a military bag of some kind.

"What the hell are you doing here?" She chomped on her lower lip as her gaze took in every inch of his six-foot-two frame. She remembered exactly what he looked like under his clothes. His thick, muscular frame hidden behind his light-blue khaki shorts, something he wouldn't have been caught dead in back in the day. Her fingers twitched, remembering his hard stomach and how she could sit for hours watching him train for baseball season. Her favorite exercises had been push-ups because she'd lie on his back, trying to distract him. It usually worked.

She let her breath out in one long swish. He hadn't changed a bit. Same light-brown hair, cut short. Same perpetual five o'clock shadow that she used to love feeling against her neck when he'd kiss her there.

"I take it you like what you see," he said, tearing her from her memories.

"You're still conceited." But he had a right to be when it came to his looks. There wasn't a girl in high school that didn't want a piece of him. But for nearly a year, she had been the lucky girl to have *every* piece of him. "You haven't answered my question."

"Are you surprised your father's not out here with a shotgun?"

"I'm sure he's looking for it," she said. Her face heated at the memory of that morning.

"The lattice is still there." He pointed to the side of the house where her personal private patio ended. "I could climb up like I used to?"

"Wouldn't want you to hurt yourself, old man."

He laughed. "Your father didn't tell you I was coming?"

She shook her head. "You can't be the guy from The Aegis Network."

"In the flesh."

"Logan Sarich," her mother's voice echoed through the thick Florida humid air. "I couldn't believe it when Brett said you were coming. You just missed your mother by an hour."

"I met her for a cup of coffee before I came here."

Mia watched her mother give Logan a hug. He stiffened when her father slammed the front door.

"Logan," her father said in a brisk tone. "Thank you for coming."

"Happy to help." Logan stretched out his hand.

Mia watched her father shake Logan's hand in a firm grip. Friendly enough, but the way her father drew his lips in a tight line indicated he'd never gotten over what he saw the morning she'd left for her first year at Poly-Tech. Based on Logan's 'at attention' stance, he was still petrified of her father.

Her father cleared his throat. "I don't know the protocol for this sort of thing."

"Best place for me to start is to interview Mia and Markus, and then I'm going to need access to all of your security system so I can evaluate any weak spots."

"Whatever needs to be done to keep my family safe." Her father rested his hand on Logan's shoulder, looking up at Mia. "Get your brother and meet us in the kitchen."

"Will do." She lingered for a moment, watching Logan as he crossed the front yard. *Damn, still the nicest ass in the state of Florida.*

She walked the long hallway toward her brother's childhood bedroom. Neither one of them had wanted to move back to their parents' house at the age of thirty-two, even temporarily. However, after finding out her own computer system had been hacked this morning, she knew it was best if her and Markus were under the same roof.

"Markus?" She tapped on the door. "The guy from The Aegis Network is here, and you're not going to believe who it is."

She waited a few moments, hearing nothing.

"Markus," she said a little louder before pushing back the door, knowing he often worked with head-phones on...in his underwear. Not a look she needed to see on her brother. She shook her head, kicking aside a couple of dirty towels that had been left on the floor, along with half the clothes he'd brought over. Her heels clicked against the floor as she strode across the room, checking his patio, but no Markus. When she turned toward the bathroom, she noticed a bottle of red wine on the floor, tipped over. Her mother would have a cow if she saw red liquid on her new white tile floors. As Mia got closer, she noticed the spill on the floor wasn't wine.

"Mom! Dad!" But it was pointless to yell in a twenty-thousand-square-foot home.

Mia knelt, getting a better look.

*Blood.*

She jerked upright, stumbling backward until her butt landed on the messy bed. "No..." She took off down the hallway toward the far spiral staircase that looped down by the kitchen, knocking at least one family portrait off the wall.

"Logan," she shouted.

By the time she got to the staircase, he stood at the bottom, hands on his hips.

"What's wrong?" he asked.

She missed the last step and fell into his strong arms, twisting her ankle. "Shit."

He hoisted her up as she leaned into his body, lacing her fingers around his massive biceps.

"Are you hurt?"

She shook her head as she kicked off her heels, tilting her chin up so she could see his face instead of his chest. "It's Markus. He's gone, and there is blood on the bathroom floor."

"What!" Her mother screeched from the other room.

Mia's chest heaved up and down as she struggled to breathe. She focused on Logan's light-green eyes as she tried to mentally stop her body from trembling.

"Calm down." Logan's hands pressed firmly against her hips, holding her steady. "Could he be anywhere else in the house?"

"Sure," Mia said as Logan raised his arm, stopping her father from passing.

"Get out of my way," her father snapped.

"We'll all go together...sir." Logan reached around her waist and hoisted her to the side with a single hand. "I'll assess the situation while we search the house together, and then we'll go from there, okay?"

She took one step on the ankle she'd twisted and groaned, grabbing Logan's hand.

"Are you going to be all right to walk?" Logan didn't wait for an answer as he looped his brawny arm around her waist. "Grab hold of my shoulder."

"I'll help my daughter," her father bellowed.

"It's all right, sir. I've got her." Logan didn't ease his grip. Her feet barely touched the ground as they climbed the staircase. "Where else does he like to go in the house?"

"Nowhere," her father said. "Even when he was in high school, he'd stay in his room for hours and tinker with computers and gadgets."

"Really, you can put me down," she whispered. A girl could get used to being carried around by a strong, viral man, but not at the expense of her father's comfort level.

"All right." But he held tight right up until they'd made their way into Markus' room. Only then did Logan gently set her on the bed.

"Is he always this messy?" Logan asked.

"Yes," her mother said, picking up a few items and folding them. "He's gone through three maids this year. I feel bad for your poor mother as we use her service for everything."

Mia watched Logan as he knelt on the bathroom

floor. He'd always been levelheaded, even as a teenager. Never partying...too much. Almost always doing the right thing, though he did enjoy bending a rule or two when it came to their sexual relationship and sneaking into her bedroom at night.

"When was the last time anyone saw him?" Logan asked.

"Lunch," Mia said, sitting on the bed, eyeing Logan and his glutes. "Then he went back to work on trying to figure out who hacked my system this morning."

Logan glanced over his shoulder. "You got hacked? This morning? Why didn't I know this?"

"I figured it could wait until you got here."

"You figured wrong." Logan stood. "That's definitely blood."

Her mother gasped.

"He could have cut himself shaving," Logan said with a reassuring tone as he pointed to a razor on the vanity. "Anyone have their phone on them? Before we panic, let's try calling him."

"I'll call him," Mia said as she tapped her phone, but it didn't even ring before going straight to voicemail. "He often lets the battery run out on his phone." Mia pointed to the empty desk. "His computer is gone."

"As I recall, he never went anywhere without that." Logan scratched the back of his head with one hand, the other one resting on his hip.

In the scope of Logan Sarich's body language, that wasn't a good sign.

"He wouldn't take his computer without taking these." Her father stood next to the desk, holding up a set of noise-canceling headphones.

"All right." Logan let out a long breath. "I'm going to make a few phone calls while we search the house. When he was younger and not in his room, where would he go?"

"He'd come hang out with me, or maybe the game room," Mia said.

Logan rubbed his scruffy face as he looked around. "You and Markus are the complete opposite. Your room was always clean as a—"

Her father cleared his throat. Loudly.

Logan glanced at her, his eyes closing briefly, and he got that scared little boy look, like her father was going to chase him out of the house with a baseball bat. Logan held out his hand.

"I can walk," she said,

Logan nodded, obviously relieved.

# Chapter Three

Logan dumped his rucksack on the bed in the pool house and glanced out the window. The beacon from the Lighthouse flashed across the darkening sky, casting an eerie glow. There were only a few houses on Jupiter Island that looked over both the ocean and the Intracoastal Waterway.

The Vanderlin home was one of them.

Mia stood next to him, heating up his body like a good cup of hot chocolate with mini marshmallows on a chilly winter morning. He hoped the A/C would kick in soon because he needed some cooling down.

"Your father still scares the shit out me."

She laughed. "You carried me up the stairs.

Don't see how you could do that if he intimidates you so much."

"Totally different. I was on the job, protecting you. He's paying me to do shit like that, not remind him of my past transgressions." He shook his hands out. "My little brother texted about a half hour ago. He's headed to your brother's townhouse now. I'm sure it's as you said, and Markus just couldn't work in your parents' home."

"We're lucky Dylan was home on leave. Please thank him for us."

"He doesn't mind." Logan did his best not to stare, but Mia Vanderlin, with her long wavy hair, airy smile, and perfect complexion commanded his attention. "You need to make your parents understand that I'm not sleeping in here, because I can't look your father in the eye again and ask."

Mia sat in the chair next to the bed, her feet resting on an ottoman, showing off her sexy, tanned legs. The first time he'd seen those legs had been their junior year. He'd been warming up, tossing a few pitches over the mound when those legs graced his vision as she ran around the outer track. He figured it had to be a new student, so the next time she made her way around the field, he made sure he stood on the side. He had the best one-liner ready. He waved to her, smiling until she stopped and pulled off her baseball cap, letting her long hair flow over her shoulders, revealing her identity as his sophomore biology lab partner from the year before.

"My mother is talking to him now, but with Markus missing, I'm not sure how well that's going to go." She'd dropped her head back on the chair, eyes closed, twirling a piece of her hair.

"They hired me to do a job, and I happen to be quite good at it."

"They both know that. When my dad called The Aegis Network, Mom said he actually smiled when he hung up the phone and told her Logan Sarich would be our protector, but seeing him with you earlier, well, I think catching us in bed scarred him for life."

"If he had come in ten minutes earlier, it would have been way worse." Logan sighed as he fell back onto the mattress and stared at the ceiling. "I don't know what was more frightening. Getting caught naked in your bed with my arms around you by your dad, or the wrath of my mother when she came to work that morning."

"We certainly surprised a lot of people our senior year," she said.

"Yeah, well, who would have thought a poor,

dumb jock like me would have hooked up with a rich geek like you." He rose up on his elbows. "You weren't the most social girl in school."

She opened her eyes, tilting her head. "You saw how people treated me. Hell, you were even standoffish."

"You terrified me," he said. "I screwed up that lab, giving you your only B, and you went off on me. I seriously thought you were going to hit me."

"I thought about it." She smiled, but the strain of the situation couldn't be hidden in her blue eyes. "My mom has always liked you."

"She tolerated me, but your dad? He always looked like he wanted to stick a knife in my heart. Besides being a poor boy who couldn't give you the life you'd been accustomed to—"

"Did he really say that?"

"Senior prom night. He took me into his office and lectured me. I almost backed out of taking you, he had me so frightened. We were seventeen. It wasn't like we were gonna run off and get married."

"Ha! That's basically what your brother Nick did."

"I'm not Nick and still, your father thought I was beneath you."

"No one will ever be good enough for me, but he did do a little happy dance when we broke up."

"That's funny." Logan winked. "Because technically we're still in a relationship."

"How do you figure that?"

He adored the way her eyes narrowed as she cocked her head in a playful gesture. "You flew off to Poly-Tech, and I went to Florida University, but neither of us ever got a chance to say it was over that day."

She kicked his leg. "We always said that at the end of our senior year we'd go our own ways. Do our own thing, never preventing the other from achieving whatever it is they wanted. It's not like we were madly in love and couldn't live without each other."

"The distance didn't help us either." He kicked off his boat shoes and ran his big toe across her muscular calf. Her smile still took his breath away. He continued to tickle her leg with his foot, enjoying the familiarity.

"Can I ask you something?" Her fingers glided through her thick hair, a habit that used to bug the shit out of him, but as more memories flooded his brain, he thought it sexy as hell.

"Shoot." He didn't expect there'd be any awkwardness with her, but he didn't predict such a strong desire to take the woman to bed, much less pick up where they had left off fourteen years ago.

"Why'd you drop out of college when you blew out your shoulder?"

"I lost my scholarship and couldn't afford it," Logan said, still staring into her eyes, remembering every curve of her body, right down to the dimple she had on her right ass cheek. She'd been the first girl he'd had sex with. The first girl he had any real feelings for, though he wasn't sure if it had been love or not, which seemed to elude him anyway. Of course, the majority of his military career, there hadn't been any time for romance.

There still wasn't time for it.

"You could have taken out a loan for the last year." The way she rolled her head to the side, locking gazes with him, sent his body into a frenzy of passion.

*Don't sleep with the client.*

He nodded, pushing himself to a sitting position, rubbing his right shoulder. "Coach kept telling me I was good enough for the major leagues, and I wanted it so bad I could taste it. After surgery, the doctor told me it would be a long recovery. I worked my ass off, but after sitting the bench my second year, my shoulder still wasn't right. So when Coach called telling me I'd essentially been replaced, I kind of lost it, and joining the Army seemed like a good idea at the time."

She dropped her legs to the floor, crossing her ankles. "I have to admit, I was a little surprised when I'd heard that."

"My mom wasn't so happy about it, especially since all three of my little brothers seem to be following my lead." He let his gaze roam from her toes to her hips to the swell of her round, perky breasts pressing against her formfitting white blouse. He'd had his share of pretty women, but seeing Mia again, well, nothing could compare.

"You can stop gawking," she said, batting her eyelashes and puckering her lips.

"I'm not—"

His phone vibrated. "It's Dylan." He tapped the green button. "Any luck?"

"Yep. He's been at his place this entire time."

"You've got to be fucking kidding me. Why?" Logan shifted, propping his head up on a few pillows.

Mia mouthed: *He found my brother?*

Logan nodded as he patted the comforter, motioning her over.

"He used a bunch of tech words I didn't quite

understand, but I deciphered enough that he needed some of his equipment," Dylan said. "He'd planned on bringing a lot of it back to his parents' but got caught up following some digital trail to whoever hacked Mia's computer."

"Can you follow him back here?" Logan asked.

"If you give me a tour of the mansion and—"

Logan cut off his baby brother. "Not happening." He tossed the phone on the bed, shaking his head. "Does your brother understand that these threats are real?"

"I'm sure he does." She curled up next to him, her knee touching his thigh, her hands tucked up under her cheek. "But he doesn't think they are after him."

"Why is that?" He glided his fingers in a circular motion across her bare shoulder.

"It was my job, not his. He only came in to help once I screwed things up."

"Screwed up how?"

"A lot of our clients will have their IT person put in some virus, or dummy security problem. I even had one client go as far as to hire an actual hacker to mess with me. So, when I was in the DANA Corps system, and I saw the file switches, I thought they were fucking with me."

"My boss told me you were threatened."

"That happened after I sent a virus that wiped out part of the hacker's system."

"If you thought it was just your client, why fuck with them by screwing up part of their system?"

"To show them that when they do something like that while I'm testing, it creates a bigger gap in cyber security. I also wanted to demonstrate to them how vulnerable they were. I just moved the files to an outside server, making it appear a virus had wiped out their system."

"When did you figure out someone else hacked into DANA Corp?"

"Three hours later when they hacked back in and threatened to kill me if I didn't give them the data."

"So that's when you decided to dummy it again, giving it to the CIA?"

"I couldn't let whoever these people were get away with it." She wrapped her arm around his middle and draped her bare leg over his thigh. "Markus didn't even know what I did, until it was too late."

"We'll find the culprits, and I'll make sure you and your family stay safe until then."

"Logan?"

"What?"

"Are you as uncomfortably comfortable as I am?"

He rolled, cupping her face, staring into her crystal-blue eyes. His heart beat faster than when he would prepare to jump from a perfectly good plane. "I'm not exactly sure what you mean."

"We don't even know each other anymore, and yet, here we are, arms and legs wrapped around each other, about to kiss as if we hadn't been apart for over a decade." She licked her plump rosy lips.

He groaned, pulling her body hard against his, wondering why he'd be willing to risk his new job, and probably his life if her father walked in again, to taste her one more time. He stared at her, searching her face for something unfamiliar. Something that told him he had no idea who this woman was anymore. But the way she smiled, with her lips slightly parted and her fingers digging into his back, all he saw was the young girl he'd never quite forgotten.

"Are you going to kiss me or what?" she whispered before she engaged his mouth with her fiery tongue.

He cupped her ass, pushing his knee further between her legs, her heat landing directly on his thigh. Hard to believe that in all his years, his first still had the ability to pull him completely from reality.

He slipped his hand under her short skirt, finding her firm, bare ass. His fingers twitched to feel her warmth wrapped around them.

She wiggled against his leg, her hand wedged between their stomachs, her fingers working their way into his shorts, snapping him back to the present. He slowed the kiss down, gently pushing her away.

"We can't do this." He cleared his throat. "Besides, the door isn't locked, and I'm not in the mood to get caught and subsequently murdered. There is the little problem of who I'm working for." He stood. "I'm your bodyguard."

"I'd say that was guarding my body." She'd rolled over on her stomach, feet in the air, her skirt not covering that damn dimple that he wanted to press his lips against.

He bent over, smoothing down the fabric and retracting his hands quickly before he jumped on top of her.

"I'm serious, Mia. My boss did some digging, and STEALTH is one badass organization that sells information, technology, and other stuff to home-grown terrorists. I can't be having a trip down memory lane with the first girl I had sex with." He shook his hands out, hoping to ease the tightness in his body. "And your father would kill me."

He must have driven his point home as her beautiful eyes went from laden to concerned.

"I'm sorry." With dignity and a sense of grace like no other woman he'd met, she rose, meeting his gaze. "I'm scared, and I think it just felt good to be in your arms again."

"I'm not going to let anything happen to you." He drew a hand down his jaw. "If you can't talk your parents into letting me stay in the main house—"

"Mia? Logan?" Her mother's voice cut through the thin walls.

"I'll let her in." Logan opened the door. "Yes, Mrs. Vanderlin?"

"Markus is back, and your brother is with him. Is it okay that I let Dylan in?"

"That's fine," Logan said, wiping his lips, hoping he didn't have lipstick plastered on his face. "But we need to discuss the new system for people coming in and out. The locks are being changed in the morning, and Mia said she changed all the passcodes."

"Your mother has a key," Mrs. Vanderlin said. "All my full-time staff does as well, and they've been with me for years. I don't understand why they can't have a key."

"Mom, it's only temporary." Mia looped her arm around her mother. "Were you able to talk any sense into Dad?"

"He's agreed. Logan can sleep in one of the guest rooms."

"I need to be on the first floor, and no bedroom is necessary. I won't be sleeping much, so a sofa will do just fine."

Mrs. Vanderlin scowled but nodded.

"Let's head over to the house. I need to talk to Markus." But what Logan really needed was some magical pill that would turn off the instant arousal he got anytime he looked at Mia.

# Chapter Four

Mia stepped into the kitchen with her mom at her side and Logan trailing behind. Her brother sat at the table, eating a bowl of something.

"You're a jerk." She smacked her brother.

"Ouch." Markus rubbed the back of his head. "Was that really necessary?"

"It was," Logan said, leaning over the table and towering over her brother. "You should be grateful it came from her and not me."

"Nice to see you too." Markus smirked, reaching his hand out. "I have to say not only was I shocked to see your brother banging on my door, but I'm stunned you're part of this Aegis Network."

"Someone has to protect your pathetic ass...sorry, Mrs. Vanderlin."

"It's fine," she said quietly. "Do you need me for anything? I think I want to go join Brett upstairs."

"Nothing tonight. We'll talk in the morning." Logan nodded.

"Night, Mom." Mia gave her mom a kiss on the cheek, hugging her a little longer than normal.

"Where's my brother?" Logan asked.

"Right here." 'Little Dylan Sarich,' who wasn't so little anymore, stepped from the bathroom.

"Oh my," she whispered, craning her neck. "You weren't that tall the last time I saw you."

"I was what? Eleven or twelve when you two graduated?" He glided across the room toward Logan.

"Nothing worse than having the baby of the family be the tallest." Logan grabbed his brother's hand in one of those bro shakes, then a huge hug with a couple of loud slaps on the back. "How's Fort Bragg treating you?"

"It fucking sucks," Dylan said. "I mean the training is going fine, but that has to be the worst fort to be stationed at."

"No one likes it there." Logan leaned against the kitchen sink. "How long are you home for?"

"A week. I pick up Nick at the airport in the

morning. Did you know he's thinking about not re-enlisting?"

"I did," Logan said, understanding Nick's desire to do something different. "I might need some help with a few things while I'm here, if you don't mind."

"Any time." Dylan waved his hand in the air. "Anything to keep Mom from setting me up on dates with her friends' kids."

Mia laughed. "That's got to be the worst."

"You have no idea." Dylan patted her shoulder as he breezed by. "It's worse for Nick. He still hasn't gotten over his wife's death, and Ramey, well, I'm hoping Mom has finally figured out he's a walking heartbreaker, and he's never going to change."

"I'm sure your mom just wants all of her boys happy." Mia twirled her hair, glancing between the two brothers.

"All she wants is a grandbaby." Dylan smiled. "I'll see myself out."

Mia pulled out a chair and sat across from her brother and glared. "You scared the crap out of me."

Markus shrugged. "I didn't think I'd be that long, but I found something before I shut down my system." He pushed a piece of paper across the table. "I wasn't sure until I ran a few more pages of code, but that's Raisin's signature."

"No way." She stared at the computer printout, but sure enough, embedded deep in the code was a small raisin and the words 'was here.'

"Who's Raisin?" Logan leaned against the kitchen counter, slicing an apple.

"A relatively well-known underground hacker." Mia continued to twirl and knot her hair. "But we don't know his true identity."

"He tries to mess with us every now and then." Markus pushed his bowl aside. "Looks like Raisin picked up some new skills."

"And a few terrorists," Logan said.

"It's possible that Raisin's attack on my computer isn't related to STEALTH." Mia shivered, mentally scolding herself. She was supposed to be the best of the best, and letting a low-level moron like Raisin into her system made her want to toss her best Jimmy Choo shoes into Jupiter Sound.

"It's too much of a coincidence," Logan said, studying his apple slice before stuffing it in his mouth. "This test you did for DANA Corp, how public was it?"

"They made an announcement that they were going to bring us in, but they delayed the actual testing twice."

"Why?" Logan scratched his scruffy cheek with the knife he used to cut his apple.

Mia shook her head, narrowing her stare. She hated it when he did that.

He just shrugged.

"They wanted the new system in place before we ran the test," Mia said, not hiding her annoyance, though she had no reason to be annoyed. He wasn't her boyfriend, and he could cut his face if he wanted to.

"What caused the delay of getting the new system installed?"

"We didn't write the system, so no idea, but it happens."

"I'll need you to send me everything you know about this Raisin person and copy my team." Logan tossed the apple core in the trash. "Our IT person is a woman named Misky Walbert. She's really good."

"Will do," Markus said, tapping his fingers on the table as if it were a keyboard. "I almost had the little bastard, but then Dylan showed up, and Raisin went for cyber cover."

"You were on the internet the entire time you were gone?" Mia blinked. "Are you really that dumb?"

"Relax, sis. I routed myself to a café in West

Palm Beach under the name Helga, which is the name I've used many times to do this exact type of shit." Markus stood and leaned against the counter, kitty-corner to Logan. The two men couldn't be more different. Markus' frame dwarfed next to Logan's, not to mention Markus' pasty skin because he rarely went outside. "I'm heading to my room and see if I can flush this guy out." Markus pointed to Mia. "Want to help?"

"The fact that I got hacked this morning on my personal computer is enough to make me shut down for a while."

"You've been shutting down a lot lately." Markus cocked his head. His eyes narrowed.

Mia couldn't argue that point. The last year, her heart hadn't been in the hacker's world. She had no idea why. The thrill of breaking through airtight cyber security had almost been better than sex, but now it bored her more than watching golf on television.

Logan tossed the knife in the sink and folded his arms. "No internet until Misky sets up a secure—"

"That's funny," Markus interrupted as he sported a toothy grin. "Especially when you have two of the world's—"

"Let me talk." Logan shook his head as he pulled

out a small military issue computer from his bag. "We're all well aware of your talents, which is why you're going to work with Misky, so you can do whatever it is you do, but you're going to do so using our coms. Got it?"

Mia ran her fingers across the thick metal before flipping it open. "You know how to use this?" She'd seen her fair share of military grade systems over the years, and for the most part, the security on these things, along with their IP-based communications, were nearly unhackable.

The key word: nearly.

Logan laughed. "My computer skills have improved over the years."

Markus snagged the computer. "I'm going to have fun with this."

"I've got another project for you." Logan leaned over the table, his knuckles on the wood top right next to her hand. It would be so easy to reach out and grab his wrist, strategically resting his palm on her breast.

"What's that?" Markus asked.

"Connect the home security system to my coms computer. That way we'll have—"

"Already ahead of you." Markus smiled. "It's really good to see you again."

"You too," Logan said, smacking Markus on the back. "But if you leave this house without me, I will hang you from the flagpole by your underwear."

Both Markus and Logan laughed as they shook hands, and it warmed her heart, remembering how Logan had come to her brother's rescue more than once, including the near date with that flagpole.

"Your friends in high school were assholes." Markus tucked the computer under his armpit.

"I was an asshole."

Markus laughed as he stepped out of the kitchen.

"He knows you're the one who dumped that jerk's motorcycle in the river after the incident with manure in Markus' car."

"I think everyone knows I did that." Logan laughed. "Including my father who constantly threatened to arrest me himself."

"Your dad was a great man. I wish I could have made it back for his funeral."

The warmness in Logan's green eyes turned sullen. His father had been a true hero and Logan's biggest fan.

"We appreciated the flowers and donation to the police department and Wounded Warrior Foundation." He ran a hand across his brown hair. "Your folks were really good to my mom and younger brothers, especially with helping Ramey and Dylan get into West Point."

"Your mom has been working here since before we were born."

"I think the last time I spoke to you was after my father died."

"On the phone for nearly four hours." Mia couldn't deny the pull she had toward him as she stood and looped an arm around his broad shoulders. "You wouldn't let me come see you the following week."

He draped his hand around her waist. "I would have loved to see you, but my girlfriend at the time didn't even like me talking to you on the phone."

"That's why you said no?"

He shook his head. "I didn't want you to come because I would have done this." With both of his hands firmly planted on her hips, he positioned her body against his. His lips parted right before he brushed them against hers in a slow, tender dance. She gripped his shoulders, raising up on tiptoe, trying to deepen the kiss, but he kept it controlled and slow, ending it all too soon. His thumbs fanned her cheeks as she stared into his intense green eyes. "What have you done to me, Mia Vanderlin?"

Her breath came in heaving pants. "I think I

should be asking you that question since I can't seem to keep my hands off you."

He patted her ass. "I didn't expect this."

"I need some fresh air," she said, fanning herself. "Care to join me on my balcony?"

"Not a good idea." He kissed her neck. "But I'll walk you to your room."

She laced her fingers though his and led him up the circular staircase. She smiled at the memories flooding her mind as she pushed open her bedroom door.

"Wow," he whispered. "This room hasn't changed much." He let go of her hand as he made his way to the sliding glass doors, passing the same canopy white bed he hid under more than once. For a man that thought her father would strangle him with his bare hands, Logan certainly took a lot of chances sneaking into her room at night.

"Do you want a glass of wine? I don't have any beer up here, but Markus might."

He shook his head. "I don't drink on the job."

"I'm going to have one." She opened her mini fridge and pulled out the bottle she'd opened last night. She kicked off her shoes before stepping out to the patio and settled into one of the lounge chairs while Logan gripped the railing, his back to her, looking at...she had no idea...but she enjoyed the view of his backside.

The crisp peach-flavored white wine tickled her throat. She reached to the side, pulling another chair close to hers. "Would you please come sit down; you're making me nervous."

He pushed off the railing and sauntered in her direction. "I need to go." He bent over, kissing her forehead. "Get some sleep. I'll see you in the morning."

She let out a long sigh, staring at the moon and the stars. "I'm really glad they sent you."

"Me too." He stepped into her bedroom, then disappeared into the hallway.

She had no idea how badly she'd missed him the last few years.

# Chapter Five

Logan stood behind Markus and his four computer screens, staring at scrolls of numbers and letters that made no sense at all while Markus pounded on the keyboard like he wanted to destroy it. "What is all of this?" Logan scratched the back of his head.

Markus adjusted his headphones, one side covered an ear, the other side pressing against his head behind the other ear. "This is everything DANA Corp and the CIA will let us have on Mia's cyber check and communication with STEALTH, along with all her analyses of the weak spots, how to fix them, and the code she wrote to wipe out the threat she thought was fake."

"You really think you can find out if this Raisin person had any part of the hack on DANA Corp?"

Markus tapped a couple of keys, which froze one screen, but the others kept scrolling. "I'm running what you would call a keyword search, only I'm analyzing the code itself. Not only do we have a unique signature, but we all have different ways of formatting the code. Think of it as handwriting or writing style."

"Easy enough." Even with the one screen frozen, Logan couldn't decipher a damn thing.

Markus zoomed in on some gibberish and pointed. "Given five thousand words, it's possible to find the author of an anonymous posting by running an analysis of similar styles. You can do the same thing with the way a programmer writes code."

"Okay." Logan huffed out some air. He appreciated Markus dumbing it down, but Logan wasn't sure he'd ever understand half of it. "Why is that important?"

"I'm doing the same thing, pulling out what I know is Mia's, or other programmers who have written code in these files." Markus tapped a few keys, and the screen flashed numbers in a window, scrolling quickly. "Over the years, we've collected patterns that Raisin tends to use, so what's left of the code, I will compare to see if it matches his, and your IT chick is taking what I can't match anywhere and comparing it to—"

"I get the picture." Logan blinked. All the numbers and letters flashing across the screen only gave him a pounding headache. "What about the security cameras?"

"All have been rerouted through your coms, and you can access them on your phone or tablet at any time. I've got the family room and kitchen TVs running live feeds. Also runs to your IT chick."

"You always manage to make me feel technologically challenged."

"Challenged is being kind." Markus tapped the keyboard, and a second screen froze.

Logan and Markus have had a weird friendship since middle school. They weren't close, but Logan had taken on the role of protector after watching some of his buddies from the modified baseball team take potshots at the computer geek. Mia, back then, barely noticed Logan. When she'd said thank you at the end of eighth grade for being kind to her brother, she looked at him as though he were an alien with five heads.

"Well, you couldn't hit a baseball with an oversized door." Logan slapped Markus on the shoulder.

"I'm going to walk the perimeter. Let me know if you find anything."

Markus nodded, adjusting his headphones, covering both ears. The heavy beat of drums pounded across the room.

Logan strolled down the hallway, glancing at Mia's door, contemplating knocking, but thought better of it when Mr. Vanderlin stepped out of the master suite at the top of the main staircase.

"Good morning, sir." Logan swallowed his breath as he gripped the railing, staring down over the massive foyer that looked more like a living room with two wingback chairs, a small armoire desk, and a hutch filled with expensive trinkets. "We've got the new security system up and running thanks to Markus."

Mr. Vanderlin stood next to Logan, holding on to the same railing. "I know my son thinks this is overkill, but the CIA seems to be taking it seriously, and so should we."

"We're in agreement on that." Logan had always been intimated by Mr. Vanderlin, but he respected him. He knew Mr. Vanderlin to be a decent man. He'd always treated his mother right, even after the 'incident.' Not once did Mr. Vanderlin take Logan's indiscretion out on his mother. But still, the man had an unnerving effect on Logan. "I do have some buddies who have done contract work for the CIA, and they are doing some digging, trying to get Markus more information to work with."

"We were told that would be impossible."

"Nothing is impossible for the people I work for." Logan ran a hand across the back of his neck, glancing at Mia's father.

"The lady at The Aegis Network said you'd be here to protect us and that the CIA would handle everything else."

Mr. Vanderlin stood stoic at the railing. The lines on his face deepened with concern.

Logan swallowed. "The best way for me to protect you and your family is to find the source, and I'm not going to sit around and wait for someone else to figure that out."

Mr. Vanderlin nodded.

"I need to go check the perimeter and see who has checked on to the property." Logan pushed from the railing and turned his back when a firm hand came down on his shoulder. "Yes, sir?" He turned, staring Mr. Vanderlin in the eye. Man to man. Showing him the respect he deserved, even though on the inside, Logan wanted to run like a small boy caught with his hand in the cookie jar.

"I was sorry to hear you lost your athletic scholarship," Mr. Vanderlin said, his glare softening. "You were a talented pitcher."

"I appreciate that." Logan's throwing arm twitched, remembering how his biceps tightened right before he released a curveball. "I loved the game. Still do. But I was meant to do other things, and life is too short to have regrets."

"Yes, it is," Mr. Vanderlin said with a slight smile. "I'll let you get to work."

Logan waited for Mr. Vanderlin to get halfway down the stairs before taking a deep breath. The embarrassment of that day would never go away. The odd part was that Logan never once regretted it. Mia made his high school days truly the best time of his life. Even striking out twelve players in his first collegiate game couldn't top that, and that was damn fucking orgasmic.

His phone vibrated. He pulled it from his back pocket and saw his mother's number flashing. "Hey, Mom," he said as he made his way down the stairs. "Are you here?"

"I am, but I have a problem."

"What's that?"

"Ida called in sick, but she didn't call me, and my

secretary called the temp agency who sent a replacement."

"We can't have a temp in here right now." Logan pushed open the front door with a little too much force. "Where are you?" The last thing he needed was a breach on the first day.

"I'm at the gate, with the temp, trying to explain—"

"I'll be right there," Logan said, taking long strides toward the road. Birds chirped and fluttered over five large feeders on the front lawn while the Florida sun beat down, causing a bead of perspiration to form on the back of his neck. He eyed Mia, lounging by the pool in a little red bikini. He groaned and waved, but kept on walking toward his mother who stood next to the gate, which was wide open. A white beat-up sedan had parked in front of the gate on the side of the road.

Logan surveyed the area, scanning for anyone or anything that looked out of place, before tilting his head so he could get a good look at the woman sitting behind the steering wheel.

"This is my son," his mother said, looping her hand around the crook of his elbow.

"I'm supposed to report to work here today," a young woman who appeared to be in her early twenties said. She had long blonde hair, tucked up in a big messy bun. "I can't get ahold of the service, and if I don't report, I will get in trouble and lose out on my pay."

"I told you my company will explain to the service the misunderstanding," his mother replied. "And pay you for the day."

"You can't make that call," the woman in the car said. "Only the owner can."

Logan laughed, glancing toward his mother who shrugged. "She's Catherine Sarich, the owner."

"That can't be possible." The girl did a double take. "Why didn't you say something?" She scowled, narrowing her eyes.

"I tried," his mother said.

"Oh." The girl slammed the gear shift. "I guess I have the day off."

Logan stepped back, wrapping his fingers over his mother's hand, still resting on his arm. "You really need to be more direct."

"That girl wouldn't let me get a word in edgewise."

"You still don't act like a boss." He tugged his mother toward the main house as the front gate closed. "And you make enough money owning the maid service that you don't have to work here anymore."

"I'm not having that argument with you," she said, waggling her index finger in his face. "Dylan already gave me the lecture last night, and I told him when one of you boys gets married and makes me a grandma, I'll think about it."

Logan shook his head and sighed. "You're running yourself ragged doing both jobs."

"Better than being bored playing bridge while everyone else talks about their grandbabies."

He did his best to keep his focus on the side door to the kitchen as he passed the pool area. The woman lying on her stomach with the little red bikini, sun-kissed skin, her chin resting on her hands, looking right at him, was too much to ignore. He smiled, giving Mia a little nod.

"She's still single." His mother squeezed his biceps.

"I'm well aware."

"Now that you're living in Orlando, you could ask—"

"I love you, Mom. But you've really got to stop playing matchmaker."

She looked up at him as he opened the back door

for her. "I just want my boys happy, and you all seem to be a little lost."

It wasn't that he and his brothers were lost. It had more to do with a restless soul. Nick had been the only one out of the four to even try settling down, but when his wife died, it nearly destroyed him. Maybe they were all just a little gun-shy.

He looked over his shoulder. Mia stood, pulling a white meshy thing over her head. Perhaps he just hadn't known a good thing when it had been right in front of him. He sucked in a deep breath and followed his mother into the kitchen.

"I'm happy." He bent over and kissed his mother's cheek.

"A good woman would be the icing on the cake."

He laughed just as Mia entered the kitchen. Her sun-drenched skin glowed in the LED lighting. The white-mesh cover-up didn't cover anything. He cleared his throat.

"Hi, Mrs. Sarich. What was that all about at the gate?" Mia asked, dumping a Kindle on the table before going to the fridge and pulling out a flavored water.

"Mix up with the temp service," his mother said, giving him that look she did when he was a kid and she wanted him to talk with someone. "I can't believe

Ida didn't call me directly. She never calls the office since she knows this is one job where we almost never use temps. Not to mention we had drinks last night, so she would have told me."

"You failed to mention that," Logan said, scratching the back of his neck. "Have you tried calling her?"

"Not yet," his mother admitted.

"Please do and let me know what you find out." Logan pulled out his phone and texted both Misky from his team and Markus about making sure they ran the plates of the temp's car. "I'll need the temp's name and address."

"I'll have to call the office for that." His mother nodded her head in Mia's direction. "I should get to work. Since Ida isn't here, I've got double the load."

It took a lot of energy on Logan's part not to roll his eyes.

"Well, you can take mine and Markus' room off the list," Mia said, leaning against the counter a little too close to where Logan had perched himself. The heat coming from her body set his skin on fire.

"I've already been told to stay clear of Markus' disaster, but are you sure about yours?"

"I'm perfectly capable of cleaning up after

myself." When Mia smiled, her eyes sparkled like diamonds.

Her hip brushed against his, and by the raised brow on his mother's face, she noticed.

"All right then," his mother said, smiling. "If you change your mind, let me know. I'll be here until three."

He counted to twenty before turning, spreading Mia's legs with his broad body, wrapping his arms around her tiny waist, and pressing his lips against hers in a tangled mess of intense lust. Darting his tongue deep in her mouth, he swirled it around, tasting a fruity beverage, which might as well have been a double shot of Fireball.

Her hands squeezed his shoulders before she dug her fingers into his flesh, dragging them down his shoulder blades, across his back, and cupping his ass.

Hoisting her up on the counter, she wrapped her legs around his waist. He managed to slip his hands under her mesh cover-up, pressing his palms against the curve of her back. Her silky-smooth skin, mixed with the coconut-scented sunscreen, allowed his hands to glide over her body, covering every inch of her exposed skin as possible.

All he could think about was removing her

bathing suit bottom and ramming himself deep inside her, leaving her begging for more.

"Logan? Oh my, well...excuse me." His mother's voice echoed across the kitchen. "Sorry to interrupt."

Quickly, he unwrapped Mia's legs and eased her between the counter and his body. She dropped her forehead to the center of his chest.

"Something wrong?" he questioned, unable to turn around, still holding Mia in his arms.

"I'm not sure," his mother said. Her voice was filled with confusion, and he wondered if it was caused by what she just saw or why she'd come back into the kitchen in the first place. "Ida just texted back saying she got a voicemail this morning not to come to work."

"From who?" Logan took in a deep breath before cupping Mia's face and looking into her wide blue eyes.

"From the office. But I never had the secretary call her, so this has me concerned."

Swallowing his pride, he kissed Mia's cheek before stepping away from her and turning to face the wrath of his mother. "I don't like the sound of that. Where is Ida now?" Mentally, he tried to force the heat of embarrassment from consuming his face.

His mother gave him that same sideways glance

she'd given him the day he'd got caught with his pants down. Her lips drawn tight, tilted head, arched brow, but if he wasn't mistaken, she also had a twinkle in her eye. "Ida decided if I didn't need her, she'd go get a mani-pedi, which is where she is right now."

Mia stayed behind Logan, her head still pressed against his back.

He reached in his back pocket for his phone, grazing Mia's midsection. "Is your secretary new?"

"She's been there about six months or so." His mother folded her arms across her chest. "Seems like a nice girl. Always on time. Polite."

"I'm going to get Dylan or Nick to come to the house. I want to go talk with Ida and your secretary." Logan didn't like the time line of when the secretary started and when Mia and her brother were hired by DANA Corp.

"Too bad Ramey couldn't come home. Ah...to have all my boys in one place. When was the last time that happened?"

"Two months ago, in South Africa." Logan laughed but immediately stopped the moment his mother gave him the evil stink eye. "Can you let Ida know I'm coming?"

His mother nodded. "What about the secretary?

I need to talk to her anyway and find out why on earth—"

"It's best you don't call her, and let me make a surprise visit." He tried to sidestep Mia, but she followed his movement, her fingers still pressed against his shoulder blades, driving him crazy.

"You think my secretary might be involved with this plot against Mia?" His mom tilted her head.

"I don't know, But I'm going to find out."

"Should I be doing anything?" His mother turned her head in the other direction, taking a step to the side.

"Business as usual." Logan reached back and tapped Mia's hip. "Go about today like you would normally do."

His mother nodded. "Mia, dear, are you going to hide behind Logan all day?"

Mia's head double thumped against his back. "No," she said meekly.

His mother smiled. "I guess I will go to work."

Mia stepped beside him.

"You two be careful where you choose to wrap yourselves around each other. We don't need another incident," his mother said as she turned and walked out of the kitchen.

Logan slowly closed his eyes, taking in a deep breath before opening them again.

"There is something wrong with us," he whispered, looping his arm around Mia and pulling her tight to his body. "Because I still want to do this." He pressed his lips against hers in a tender kiss.

She fisted her hands and pounded them on his chest. "Sex," she said, her breathing labored. "We need to have sex. Get it out of our system. Then *this* won't keep happening."

He laughed. "With our luck, the entire town will walk in on us."

# Chapter Six

Mia adjusted her baseball cap as she followed Logan into the small office of Hunter's Maid Service, named after the original owners who'd hired Logan's mother thirty plus years ago. Mrs. Sarich's first assignment had been the newly married Vanderlins, and from the very first cleaning, they'd insisted Catherine and Ida be the only housekeepers they sent. Eventually they hired the duo full time, but after Mrs. Sarich's husband died, she took a part-time position, which resulted in her deciding to purchase the agency.

"May I help you?" A young redhead sat behind a large metal desk, pencil in hand with an open textbook, her mouth gaping open as she had the nerve to give Logan the once-over.

"My name is Logan Sarich and I'd—"

The girl dropped her pencil. "Your mother isn't here right now, and I don't expect her in until three thirty."

"I know," Logan said with a tight tone. "She sent me to get some information for her."

"What do you need?" The girl leaned back in her chair, folding her arms.

"What's your name?" he asked.

"Bonnie." The redhead narrowed her eyes, glaring at Logan.

Mia glanced at Logan, who stared back at the girl with a tight jaw.

"You told Ida not to go to work. Why?" Logan sat in one of the chairs across from the desk, so Mia followed his lead.

For the first time, Bonnie looked in Mia's direction, but not for long. "Someone from the Vander-whoever's place called stating they only needed Mrs. Sarich today."

"It's Vanderlin," Mia said with an even tone. "And who specifically called?"

"I think her name was Mia," Bonnie said. "And I remember the caller ID came up with that name as well."

"That's Mia." Logan pointed. "She didn't call

you. So let's try this again. Why did you tell Ida not to go to work this morning?"

Bonnie sat up taller, tugging at her blouse as if to close it. "I told you. I got a call."

"On the office phone?"

Bonnie nodded.

"Let me see the phone," Logan barked.

Bonnie didn't waste any time pushing her chair back and standing. "You can scroll on the small screen to see who called and when."

Logan stood, towering over the petite redhead. "I hate these fucking things," he muttered. "Mia?"

"Sure thing." Mia made her way to the other side of the desk, then picked up the receiver and hit the arrow button, scrolling through numbers until hers came up. "That's my home phone." She held it up for Logan to see. "I did *not* make that phone call."

"I think you owe me an apology," Bonnie said.

Logan planted his hands on his hips and turned. "Explain to me why you called the temp agency for a replacement and sent them to the Vanderlin home."

"Excuse me?" Bonnie screeched. "I did no such thing! You've got some nerve—"

"Give me the number to the service." Logan let out a long breath before turning around. "I apologize, but we've got a situation, and I don't have time for games."

Bonnie narrowed her eyes. "You're a jerk," she said under her breath.

Mia ignored the statement and sat down behind the desk and rolled out the keyboard tray.

"What are you doing?" Bonnie asked. Her scowl deepened.

"I set this system up for Mrs. Sarich, and I know most requests for temps are done through a portal." Mia pulled up the terminal, entered her information, and then the program she wanted opened. "Nothing here indicated a request was made."

"I still want to call," Logan said, holding his phone up. "Number? Please? Anyone?"

"It's speed dial five." Bonnie stepped back. "I need to use the bathroom. Is that okay with you?"

"Yes," Logan said sharply.

Once Bonnie closed the unisex door, Mia said, "What is your problem?"

"You don't recognize her?"

"She's what, twenty-five tops? Why would I know her...oh...she's Rock's little sister, isn't she?" Mia almost never thought about Rock, who'd been the bane of her and her brother's existence. Rock had made it his mission to sabotage every science or technological project Mia and her brother did in high school, even after Rock had been transferred to private school.

Logan placed his hand on her shoulder, leaned over, and snagged what looked like a nameplate. He held it up and read the name: "Bonnie Rockmann."

"That's no reason to be mad at her." Mia hit star five, and it rang once.

"Gypsy Temp Agency. This is Kia. How may I direct your call?"

"Hi, Kia, this is Bonnie over at Hunter's Maid Service. Someone sent a temp to a job of ours today, only we didn't call for one, and I thought I'd give you a heads-up before anyone got in trouble."

"Oh dear," Kia said. "Let me check. Can you hold?"

"Sure thing."

"That's scary how well you pulled that off." Logan squeezed her shoulder.

The phone clicked. "Hi, Bonnie. This is weird. We have no work order for any maid temp today anywhere."

"Huh," Mia said. "Maybe I have the wrong temp agency. Thanks for your time." Mia hung up the phone and took Logan's hand who hoisted her out of the chair. "I want to remotely access your mom's system."

"You think she was hacked?"

Mia arched her brow. "I didn't make that call this morning, and my system was hacked."

The sound of a toilet flushing and water running reminded Mia that Bonnie was still in the office. "You really didn't need to be so mean to her."

"Yeah, I did," Logan said.

Bonnie stepped into the office. "I was hoping you two had left."

"We're heading out right now." Logan took Mia by the biceps. "Thanks for the help."

"My pleasure," Bonnie said with a spoonful of sarcasm laced with a bucket of snobbery.

Logan practically dragged Mia to the Jeep before opening the passenger door.

"You need to explain your rudeness," Mia said.

"I should have told my mother what that little bitch did." He slammed the door shut.

It took a lot for Logan to call anyone a nasty name. He generally let things go quickly, or things simply rolled off his back. So, whatever this chick did, it had to be bad. Mia touched his arm as he turned the key in the ignition. "What did she do?"

"When Dylan was seventeen, he dated her.

About a month into it, she started sending him naked selfies."

"That's all the rage these days."

He glared at her as he looked over his shoulder to pull out of the parking space. "Dylan participated as well."

"I sent you a naked picture a few times."

Logan punched the gas and the tires spun, burning rubber as the Jeep skidded into traffic. "When Dylan broke up with her, she went a little pyscho, hacking into his Facebook account and posting a few naked shots of him."

"Wow. That's crazy."

"I had to call Markus to help get them down and see if we could prove she did it, but Markus said it came from the IP address from our home so we couldn't prove it was her, but Markus managed to mess with her just enough that she went away, for good."

"You called Markus and not me?" Now that hurt.

"I intended on calling you, but Markus was home, and he said you were in the Bahamas with some dude. I think he called him the Dicky Dude, whatever that means."

She laughed. "That was Dicky Fargo. Neither Markus nor my parents liked him very much."

"Markus said your taste in men went south after I left, and he didn't think you could go any lower than me." He glanced her way and winked.

She smiled, warmth spreading across her stomach. "So what happened in the end with naked photo saga?"

"Dylan took one on the chin, saying he 'accidently' posted them. He didn't want to stir any more trouble. My poor mother. Not a single Sarich boy managed to get through school without getting caught with their pants down."

Mia scowled. "You should have nailed the little hussy."

He patted her leg. "I was more concerned with my baby brother. It was horrifying when your father walked in on us; I can't imagine what it must have felt like to have some girl post a picture of your... Well, what was worse was to have your mother think you did it."

"I think they both equally suck in different ways." She laced her fingers through his. "But I never regretted being with you, ever. I think I'd like to be with you again."

"When this assignment is over, I might be down

with that." He flashed a grin as he turned into her condo parking lot. "For old time's sake."

"I hope it's over soon, because I really don't want to wait."

He groaned. "What building is yours?"

"Building 3."

"That's the one right on the water, yes?" The Jeep rolled over a couple speed bumps, sending his hand a little closer to the edge of her mini skirt.

"It is." She released his hand, setting it back down on her inner thigh while she stretched her arm out, placing her hand on his, sliding her fingers under his shorts. "No one is going to walk in on us here."

Once parked, he turned, cupping her face and kissing her lips. "Someone managed to call from your phone. I don't think your condo is safe for anything."

"Oh." She frowned. "But that could have been done remotely."

"Maybe, but it doesn't matter." He leaned across her, opened his glove box, and pulled out a gun.

"Is that really necessary?"

"Yep." He hopped out of the Jeep. "Stay close behind me, got it?" He did something with the gun, then held it down at his side.

"You're going to scare my neighbors." She gripped his strong biceps with one hand, squeezing the bulging muscle as it flexed. She reached in her small clutch purse. "It takes two keys to get into my condo."

"So?"

"You're overreacting."

He snatched the keys. "You're trying to make light of the situation because deep down, you're scared, and you don't like admitting any kind of weakness."

He had her there, and it felt good to know he still understood the way she handled most situations. They rode the elevator to the fifth floor, which happened to be the top floor, in silence. She continued to grip his arm, and he still held his gun.

"When was the last time you were in here?" he asked, pushing her behind him as the elevator doors dinged open.

"Three days ago."

"Which apartment?"

She gripped his hips; a mixture of fear and anger prickled her skin like sandpaper. Everyone was vulnerable in the cyber world, even her. But she didn't like admitting it, much less having to deal with any ramification that came with a cyberattack. "Second door."

Logan pushed the key in, and the door swung

open without him turning it. "Did you by chance leave it unlocked?"

"You know me better than that." She fisted his shirt, ducking her head behind his back. "Do you think anyone is in there?"

"Shhh," he said. "Stay close."

He held the gun out with both hands, crouching down, taking small steps.

Her pulse beat against her throat, making it difficult to swallow.

Logan opened the pantry door, then slinked toward the guest bedroom, which doubled as her home office. However, unlike her brother, she didn't feel the need to spend her evenings in front of a dozen computer screens, so she had only one. "Does anything look out of place?" he whispered.

She peered over his shoulder, scanning the guest room. Her desk sat clutter free under the window that overlooked the Intracoastal, the Jupiter Lighthouse off to the left. Normally, her laptop would be perched on the center next to one monitor, but she'd taken her personal computer to her parents. "There should be some files in my desk drawer."

"Let's take a look then." He patted her hip, nudging her in front of him. "It's okay. You can let go of my shirt."

This condo had always been her sanctuary. The one place she could kick back, have some wine, and not feel like she had to be plugged in all the time. She tiptoed across the room, looking over her shoulder a few times, waiting for some crazy person to jump out and scare the crap out of her.

"I'm right here, baby."

"Since when do you call me baby outside of screwing my brains out."

"Since right now."

She swallowed, hoping the teasing would make her feel at ease as she pulled open the top drawer. Her notebooks were neatly stacked on the left side, and on the right side was her pen and pencil divider, organized by type and color. The next drawer contained all her hanging files, organized alphabetically by category. It dawned on her that being a neat freak was just as bad as her brother's inability to pick his dirty underwear off the floor.

"Nothing's missing."

"Let's move on to your bedroom." Logan kept his weapon raised. She gripped his white T-shirt once again as she followed him into the small master bedroom. He peeked into the walk-in closet and master bathroom.

No one anywhere to be found.

"Nice view of the inlet, except for the bridge."

"Yeah, well, if I *had* to move back here, I wanted to look at the Lighthouse."

"I kissed you for the first time there. Asked you to the prom there. Hell, we did everything except have sex at the Lighthouse." He laughed. "Why did you *have* to move back here?"

"Three years ago, my father was diagnosed with cancer." She blinked a few times, remembering how the tears stung the day her mother called to tell her the bad news.

"I'm sorry." Logan cupped her face, his thumb fanning her cheek. "How is he now?"

"Cancer free for the last year, but I'm not ready to move back to the West Coast. Besides enjoying my parents' company, I've been restless since my dad got sick."

"Understandable." Logan dropped his hand. "Anything missing in here?"

She took her time opening drawers and scanning her closet for missing items. It was pretty easy to tell nothing had been disturbed considering how orderly her life had been. She squelched the urge to knock everything in her medicine cabinet over.

Logan leaned against the window, staring at the Lighthouse, his arms folded across his chest.

"Penny for your thoughts."

"I keep going back to Bonnie. Why would she go to work for my mother?"

"Maybe she needed a job, money."

He looked over his shoulder with an arched brow. "Considering what she did, doubtful. Besides, her family is well-off."

Mia stepped around her bed, then rested her hand on his shoulder. "My parents wouldn't give Markus and me a dime to start our company. Not even a loan. We had to take one out from a regular bank. Imagine that." She tugged his arm, draping it over her shoulder.

"You and Markus always understood the value of a dollar and weren't spoiled little rich kids like Rock was." Logan kissed her temple. "Have you seen him? Know where he is?"

"No. And I don't want to."

"I want to find out where he's been. Too many coincidences lately."

"You think he's part of this?"

"He was smart, like you and Markus, so, yeah, maybe." Logan pushed away from the window. "Let's get out of here before I do something crazy like toss you on that bed and take you seven different ways." He took one step, then stopped and glanced back out the window before pulling out his phone and tapping the screen.

"I'm not opposed to that." She squeezed his ass.

He groaned. "I'm well aware, but it's going to have to wait."

She sighed. "Why? That's a perfectly good bed; we're alone—"

"I don't think we are." He shoved his phone back in his pocket.

"What!?" Her pulse sped up as she tightened her grip around his waist.

"See that white crossover car parked in the lot in front of the building next to this one?"

She scanned the cars until she found the one he described. A woman wearing jeans and a black shirt leaned against the driver's door. "What about it?"

"I saw the same car when we pulled out of my mom's office."

"That can't be good," she said.

"Let's go." He tugged her by the hand.

"What are we going to do?"

"Act like we don't know we're being followed."

She didn't like the sound of that, but she followed him through the condo building, down the elevator, and to his car where he buckled her into the passenger seat. Her body trembled as she clasped her hands in her lap, fiddling with her nails. "I think I might rather walk."

"Just safety precautions." He buckled himself to the seat, gun on his lap, then fired up his Jeep, ramming it into reverse. "That girl is definitely tailing us."

She grabbed the dashboard as the Jeep lurched forward. "This feels like we know we're being followed."

He laughed. "I always drive like this."

"You have a point." She swallowed, resisting the urge to glance over her shoulder. "Being the chief of police's kid did give you some liberties."

"Not as many as I would have liked." Logan raised part of his ass off the seat. "Get my phone. I'm getting a text, so read it to me."

"What's your passcode?" Her fingers trembled. You knew things weren't rosy when Logan got so serious he couldn't crack a smile when anyone made a funny.

"It's 051385."

Now her hands trembled for a different reason. "That's my birthday."

"Huh." He glanced her way, no smile, but his eyes conveyed the understanding of what that *could* mean. "Hold on."

She gripped the phone in one hand, while the other pressed against the side of the Jeep. "It's from Nick, and he says take her over the bridge by the Lighthouse, and he'll cut her off there."

"Text him back 'that works.'"

She did as instructed, but her fingers fumbled, and it took longer than usual. "Where should I put your phone?"

"Hold on to it in case Nick needs to reach us, or vice versa."

Logan weaved in and out of traffic, constantly looking in his rearview mirror, but looking like he didn't have a care in the world. She held her breath as they crossed over the bridge and took the right turn by the Lighthouse, eyeing Nick sitting in a beat-up old pickup.

Mia couldn't help herself as she looked over her shoulder, seeing the small white SUV taking the turn. Seconds later, tires squealed as Nick pulled his truck out in front of the car that had been trailing them. The SUV slammed right into the back of Nick's vehicle.

"Oh, my God! We should stop. Nick could be hurt."

"He's fine." Logan leaned across her and put his

weapon in the glove box as he rounded a corner right before the next bridge to the Island.

"Did he plan it that way?" She shook her hands out, then rubbed them on her legs. She'd thought some excitement in her life might help with her lack of passion for her job these days, but this was not the kind of adrenaline rush she craved.

"Pretty much." Logan slowed as they passed onto Jupiter Island. The afternoon sun beat down, and young girls walked the main drag in bikinis with barechested men, heading toward small beaches on the Intracoastal side. "He called a buddy of his still on the police force, who will be the first on the scene. This way we can get as much information about who has been tailing us."

"That's abuse of power, and probably illegal, isn't it?"

"So is hacking into the school system, changing a few of my unexcused tardies to excused, and probably erasing some of them so I could attend the prom."

She laughed. "Well, that dress I bought needed to be worn and seen, and no way was I going stag."

"That dress gave me an instant hard-on."

"I still have it, and I think it fits." The shoulder strap snapped tight as he took the turn into her driveway a little too fast. "You're very good at redirecting the conversation."

"I just don't want you to worry too much." He helped her from the Jeep.

"I'm scared to death," she admitted, hugging her middle as he looped an arm over her shoulders, guiding her to the front door. "Being followed. You with a gun. Not to mention someone threatening to kill me. It's a bit much to take in."

"Once we get a chance to talk to the chick who followed us, we should have a better handle on things."

"So, what now?" She looked around the empty yard. Weird not to have a ton of people working the grounds. Her mother must be going nuts as she liked to garden, but never alone. That gardener and his team were her mother's best friends.

"I need to talk to Dylan and check in with Nick. I also need to sit down with your brother and talk to my team." His warm lips sizzled against her cheek. "Why don't you go take a bath. Or sit down with your feet up."

"I'm not a fragile little girl."

"I never said you were." He opened the door, letting her into the refreshing air-conditioned house. "But right now, I want you inside this house. If you want to help your brother and my IT person, have at it." He pulled his phone out of his pocket and stared at it with a puzzled expression. "Don't go on the balcony, okay? Everyone stays inside."

"You're scaring me."

"Someone broke into your condo, messed with your phone, and who knows how many other people might be following...watching. Until I know more." He batted her nose. "You're staying inside or at my side."

"I like the latter."

He shook his head. "When this is over, we're going to..." He paused, blinking a few times before clearing his throat. "Mr. Vanderlin," Logan said. "May I have a word with you?"

"Of course," her father said.

She leaned against the front door, watching Logan and her father walk down the long hallway to her father's office.

While she desperately needed Logan Sarich in the most primal way, the moment this case ended, he'd be heading back to Orlando and whatever other assignments the Aegis gave him and she'd be... She shuddered, not wanting to think that far ahead.

# Chapter Seven

Logan sat in the same chair he had all those years ago when he thought it would be a good idea to ask permission to take Mia to prom. The same chair the night he picked Mia up for the prom, and the same chair the morning Mr. Vanderlin ordered him to 'get dressed, go to Mr. Vanderlin's office, and wait for his mother.'

The chair hadn't become any more comfortable fourteen years later.

Logan cleared his throat and did his best to keep eye contact with Mr. Vanderlin, who leaned forward in his chair, arms pressed against the giant desk.

"I wanted to give you an update on a couple of things," Logan said.

"I appreciate that." Mr. Vanderlin didn't blink.

"The woman that showed up saying the temp agency called is a woman by the name of Jessie Marlin. Does the name ring a bell?"

"Can't say that it does."

"Nick has one of his old cop buddies stopping by to ask her a few questions, so hopefully I'll have some information about that shortly."

"Thanks." Mr. Vanderlin still didn't bat an eyelash while he stared at Logan.

"I need to ask you a question." Logan pulled out his phone. He wanted to make sure he got the information correct. "Mia set up your financial security system, right?"

"She did a summer internship with the company that updated our banking cyber protection system, as well as many other banks."

"But she worked on it, correct?" Logan focused on the job and his training. Not the father of the woman he'd 'deflowered.'

"I don't know how much, but yes, that's correct."

"Your financial institution was recently the target of a cyberattack, but you didn't have Mia or Markus help with the situation. May I ask why?"

"I take it you didn't bring this up with my daughter."

"I wanted to ask you first."

Mr. Vanderlin leaned back, clasping his hands behind his head. "You've always been mostly respectful; I'll give you that."

"Mostly?" Logan regretted the single word question the moment it left his mouth.

Mr. Vanderlin arched a brow.

"Let's go back to the cyber threat."

Mr. Vanderlin's eyes narrowed, but he didn't look like he wanted to hang Logan in a public lynching. That had to mean something. "It was Mia and Markus who suggested we use a different company, considering the family ties, but they oversaw everything, and then they made sure our system and customers were indeed safe."

"Two of your higher employees were fired after making allegations that Mendon Cyber Security purposely installed a weakened system, leaving you and your customers vulnerable and—"

"I know where you are going with this. Yes, Mia worked for them during the installation." Mr. Vanderlin unclasped his hands, leaning forward. "You really think Mia would be so careless?"

"No." Logan swallowed, unable to break eye contact, feeling like a scared little boy. "I know she and Mendon Cyber Security were cleared of any wrongdoing before it ever made the news."

"Then why are you bringing this up?"

"I'm wondering if someone, like those two employees, had it in for Mia."

"I suppose that's possible." Mr. Vanderlin pulled open his lower drawer and placed a folder on the desk. "It's never been easy for Mia. Between having a brilliant mind, being my kid, and what that represents, she's had to deal with jealousy all her life. Unfortunately, one of those employees that I had to let go had nothing to do with the accusation. That happened after I fired her."

"May I ask why you let her go?"

"She was stealing from me." Mr. Vanderlin tapped the file. "It's all right here. I didn't press charges and regretted that decision ever since."

Logan opened the file, shocked to see Theresa Pennington's picture. "She was Rock's girlfriend back in high school."

"The same Rock that picked on Markus and..." Mr. Vanderlin fisted his hands. "He transferred to another school, right?"

Logan nodded. "I'm not liking all these connections to the past." Logan scratched the back of his neck. "While STEALTH is still our main focus right now, this underlying layer of someone out to destroy

Mia concerns me just as much." He held up the file. "Can I keep this?"

Mr. Vanderlin nodded.

"Is there anything else I need to know?"

"I can't think of anything, but if I do, I'll let you know."

"Thanks." Logan rose, extending his hand.

"Mia didn't have much of a social life until she started dating you," Mr. Vanderlin said as he took Logan's hand in a firm grip, then released it.

Logan held his breath.

"You put a smile on her face that no one else could, and I think in part, because of you, she's the confident woman she is today."

Logan let his breath out slowly. "I had nothing to do with that."

"I beg to differ." Mr. Vanderlin walked around his desk and patted Logan on the back. "It's not that I didn't like you, Logan. I wouldn't have sat through all those baseball games with my daughter if I thought you weren't good for her." Mr. Vanderlin opened the office door.

Logan stood there, staring, unable to utter a single word.

"But I wanted her to chase her dreams just as I

wanted that for you as well. You had so much talent and a full ride; that's a big deal."

"Yes, sir, it was. Unfortunately, the injury put an end to that."

"I'm truly sorry you lost your scholarship." Mr. Vanderlin lowered his chin and arched a brow. "You're a good man, and I think I've been treating you poorly because of one incident and not the entire picture."

"I appreciate that," Logan managed to reply with a high-pitched sound like he'd just hit puberty. "I want you to know that I cared a great deal about Mia... I still do."

"That's apparent." Mr. Vanderlin ushered Logan into the hallway.

"That was weird," Logan whispered after the door to the office clicked closed.

Mia glanced up over her Kindle, hearing footsteps coming down the hallway toward her bedroom.

Her mother appeared at the door.

"Hey, Mom."

"Mind if I come in for a bit?" Her mother made herself comfortable on the other wingback chair next to Mia, giving them both a good look at the ocean. "Are you okay?"

Mia set the Kindle on the coffee table. "I'm holding it together."

"You always do that, but it had to have been scary, knowing someone was in your place."

"It was...it is." Mia had never been good at showing emotion, keeping it tucked up under her sleeve. She never wanted the mean girls to know how they affected her, but with her parents, she wanted to protect them from the pain that had been her childhood. "I think I was more freaked out by Logan carrying a gun."

"I don't like having that thing in the house, but it's necessary." Her mother leaned in, placing a protective hand over Mia's. "I'm worried about you and have been long before all this other stuff happened."

Her mother had always had the ability to read Mia's emotions and moods, but she didn't always express them, letting Mia figure things out on her own. That used to bother Mia, but not anymore. Her mother gave her a gift by forcing her to either figure it out or ask for help. It was rare her mother had to push like this.

"My head hasn't been in the game for a while,"

Mia said, twirling her hair. "I find no joy in what I do anymore. I think I'm burnt out."

"Your brother would agree," her mother said, leaning back. "Only he says he's been watching you slowly back away since your father's illness."

Mia closed her eyes. "It started before that." If Mia was being totally honest with herself, her restlessness started the moment she'd graduated from college. But she dived right into starting her business with her brother, and for a while, her heart raced with the same passion she'd had when she first went to Poly-Tech, or the year she spent in Logan's arms.

"Are you unhappy?"

"No." Mia opened her eyes and rolled her head. "But I'm not completely happy either."

"Do you think you're missing something in life?"

"I don't know, but having Logan around is making me crazy, and I can't figure out why he affects me so much. It's not like we've kept in touch over the years."

Her mother smiled. "Maybe he's why you've always been restless."

"What does that mean?" Heat flashed across Mia's cheeks.

"Logan became your best friend. He was your

world, and he also brought you out of your shell. I don't think you would have made it at Poly-Tech—"

"I graduated top of my class, and I did that all on my own."

"That's not what meant." Her mother shifted. "Come sit here."

Mia slid to the floor and snuggled in between her mother's legs while her mother's fingers glided through her hair. When she was in grade school, she rarely got invited to a birthday party, so when her mother knew she'd been left out, she always made a point to spend the day either shopping, or going to the salon, or just hanging out watching old movies, braiding Mia's hair.

"You struggled socially, and we worried you wouldn't be able to leave home. Three weeks before school started your senior year, Logan knocked on the door to pick you up for your first date. Your father did his rendition of the happy dance the moment the two of you pulled out of the driveway." Her mother grabbed Mia's shoulders and shook her.

"No way. Daddy was so mean to Logan that day. Every day." She rested her cheek against her mother's thigh. "I was so embarrassed, but Logan took it in stride."

"Because Logan was a good boy, and he's turned into quite the man."

"I wish Dad would stop giving him the evil eye. He might not like Logan, but—"

"Your father likes Logan. Always has."

"He sure has a funny way of showing it," Mia muttered.

"Well, right now, he's worried about our safety."

"That's an excuse for him to be a jerk because of what happened years ago."

"That's not true. You and Logan became insepa-rable, and he would have hated it if Logan gave up his shot at the major leagues and college for you. And vice versa for your dreams. Young love can be intoxicating."

"Logan and I weren't in love." Mia let out a long sigh.

"Are you sure about that?" Her mother kissed her forehead.

Mia laughed. "Logan and I promised we'd never get in each other's way. We wanted each of us to have everything."

"Oh, honey, that's love." Her mother wrapped her arms around Mia. "I suspect you never stopped loving him, and that is why you are so restless, but the practical side of you sees the man and what he's made of himself, and you think he'd be giving some-thing up to be with you."

Mia's skin tingled with goosebumps. "That's a stretch."

"Logan's a good man, but he's lost, and I suspect that started before his father died."

Mia hugged her mother's leg, much like she did when she'd been a little girl. "You're trying to tell me that Logan and I have been in love with each other all this time?"

"Tell me this, little one. How does he make you feel now?"

"Like I'm the most special person in the world." Mia left out the most desirable as well. "It is like we've never been apart."

"I'd say that's worth exploring."

Mia tilted her head, looking up at her mother. "Daddy would have a heart attack."

"That's where you're wrong." Her mother smiled. "It's hard for a dad to actually see his little girl all grown up. The morning he found Logan in your room drove that point home."

"That was so embarrassing for Logan, and Dad is still rubbing it in his face."

Her mother laughed. "Did you ever think half of that is a game your father is playing to make sure

Logan understands that you loved your father before you loved Logan?"

"No." Mia scrunched her face.

"Your father admires and respects Logan. If he didn't, he wouldn't have sought out his help."

"What do you mean by that?" Mia twisted her body, staring at her mother. "Dad didn't know Logan worked for..."

Her mother smiled, nodding.

"Daddy knew?"

"He specifically asked for Logan."

# Chapter Eight

Logan leaned back on the sofa in the side patio and stared up at the skylight. The moon and stars danced in the dark sky. Thick, puffy white clouds drifted casually across the window.

Markus sat across the room in a wicker chair with matching ottoman, where he had set up his laptop. "STEALTH isn't taking any credit for the hack on DANA Corp." Markus' earphones now covered only one ear.

How he managed to hold a conversation with music barreling into one side of his head, Logan had no idea. "That doesn't mean anything."

"Actually, it does." Markus ripped off his headphones, tossing them on the table next to him. "You're IT person has quite an extensive file on that group, and they've never let anyone else take credit for anything they've done."

"But we're giving them credit." Logan kicked off his shoes and put his feet up, clasping his hands behind his head.

"And they are denying the hack. If it were them, they'd be shouting it across cyberspace. Not only that, I've read pages and pages of the original cyber-attack on DANA Corp, and it doesn't add up."

"What do you mean, exactly?" Logan pinched the bridge of his nose. He'd always enjoyed Markus' company, just not when he got his computer geek on.

"I've been following the flow of the stolen infor-mation, along with how the hackers replaced the data. It's not very sophisticated, and what bothers me more is that the cyber trail ends in Canada. Who the fuck routes top-secret defense plans to fucking Canada?"

"Don't they route it all different places, so you can't trace it?"

"Sure, but one of the things Mia and I do is embed code that can be traced when we do work for any government agency. It's why they use us. Mia's trail ends in Canada. Then there is the 'no chatter' problem. Usually, people talk before and after. The attack on DANA was quieter than a mouse."

Logan rubbed his unshaven face. "No intel on buy/sell of the data?"

"Nothing," Markus said.

"So, if it's not STEALTH, which would be a good thing, then who?"

Both men said, "Raisin."

"But why?" Logan asked.

"Well, I suspect to ruin Mia," Markus said, his leg bouncing up and down, rattling the floor. "Every time he came at us, it was more Mia than me. In college, he managed to hack into the school system, changing some of Mia's work and plagiarizing someone else. Took us a couple of weeks to straighten things out, but it nearly cost Mia an award and could have gotten her kicked out of school."

"How do you not know who this Raisin guy is?"

"Most hackers are anonymous because most of them aren't ethical. They are usually a recluse with little or no friends. An invisible person even when visible. Or they might have a different persona on line."

"Do you have a different persona?"

"Both Mia and I will use different names depending on the situation." Markus tapped on his computer. "We're often looking for hackers wanting to do damage, so sometimes we end up in the underground world, poking around."

"But if you each have a signature, won't people know it's you?"

"On these sites, we act like wannabes, playing stupid."

"Mia doesn't know how to play stupid."

"She's gotten better at it." Markus shut down his laptop. "But it's been a while since we've had to go underground."

"What do you think about Theresa having worked for your father and blaming Mia for the cyber threat?"

"Other than she was Rock's girlfriend until he disappeared, I don't think anything of it."

"Where is she now?"

"No idea, but we can find out."

Logan dropped his hand to his chest, tapping the center with his forefinger. "Mia seems disinterested in the cyber world. Why is that?"

"I really don't know." Markus stood. "She's been restless for a while. I thought the DANA Corp job might help her get her groove back. Between the hack, the threat, and you being back, she's even more distracted than before."

"It's definitely been a trip being in this house and

seeing her again." Logan thumped his chest to the beat of his heart. He understood restless. He'd been that way most of his life. "You think she's just bored? Wanting something different in life? Pretty much why I keep changing jobs every six years."

Markus shook his head. "I think she did what she thought she was supposed to be doing. What had been expected of her, instead of following the faint whisper in her heart that told her she wanted something else."

"And what's that?"

Markus burst out laughing. "Seriously? You both have always had your heads in the sand." With that, Markus strode out of the room, leaving Logan to wonder about things he never let himself wonder about, until his phone rang.

"Hey, Nick, tell me some good news." Logan put in his earbuds, then tapped his phone, pulling up a few images of Mia that had been in the case file.

"Don't know if it's good or bad, but it's interesting."

"Lay it on me."

"The chick I let smash my old pickup was hired for a few hundred bucks a day to follow Mia."

"By who?"

"Says she doesn't know, some woman with a fake blonde wig in a bar a few months ago," Nick said.

"She's been following her that long?" Logan bolted upright.

"Not every day. She gets texts with a schedule and is to report who Mia's with and where she goes. But the interesting part is that she was given a key by this woman the other day and told to make a phone call from Mia's apartment."

"Well, I'll be damned." A text from Mia flashed on his screen.

*Where r u? Haven't seen you in hours...*

He smiled. "Do me a favor and see what you can dig up on Rock and his ex-Theresa."

"Sure thing. Talk tomorrow."

Logan pulled the buds out of his ears and tapped the text thread from Mia.

*Side porch and have interesting news*

. . .

He was getting ready to send her a text with all the intel when she responded.

*Come to my room and tell me*

Without thinking, he typed:

*Only if u wear that dress...*

The moment he hit send, he regretted it. Well, no, he didn't. However, this wasn't going to be the brightest thing he's ever done, but it might be the most exciting thing in a long time.

He pulled up Dylan's text thread.

*You good to watch the perimeter for the next few hours?*

. . .

Logan took the steps slowly, staring at his phone. It seemed like an eternity before his brother responded.

*Sure...why?*

*I need to talk to Mia, fill her in on a few things.*

*Fill her in? Yeah, don't get caught.*

Logan shook his head, shoving his phone in his pocket while tiptoeing down the hallway. He gripped the door handle to Mia's room and sucked in a breath. Quickly, but quietly, he turned the knob and pushed back the door, closing it gently and twisting the lock. He shook the door, just to make sure it had been secured.

Terrified or not of her father, Logan needed Mia.

"Logan?" Mia stepped from her gigantic walk-in closet he'd been intimately familiar with as a halfway decent hiding place. The light spilled out into the dark room, casting a shadow on her face, but lined her perfect body with curves everywhere a woman should have them, especially in that red strapless dress. What little cleavage she did have was enhanced by her mounds being pushed out of the top of the dress. Her tiny waist looked even thinner between her breasts and hips.

"Fuck," he whispered, staring at her feet that were tucked into four-inch red heels that had been stained to match the dress.

"Will you zip me up?"

"Screw that." He closed the gap, ripping his shirt off and tossing it to the floor. "Drop that dress, baby."

"What? No foreplay?" She lifted her hands to the sides, and the red fabric pooled at her feet.

He growled. "There will be plenty of foreplay."

Her nipples puckered as he fanned his thumbs over them, then glided his hands across her stomach to her back, cupping her bare ass.

"Lots of foreplay on one condition." He hoisted her up, her legs wrapping tightly around his waist. Her fingers digging into his back, nails scraping his skin with an electric sizzle.

"What's that?"

"You leave those goddamned shoes on."

"I'll do that if you take these pants off. Not a good feeling against my clean-shaven you-know-what."

He groaned again, dropping her to the bed while he stood at the end, undoing his belt. "You still can't say that word, can you?" He smiled.

"If you say it, all bets are off." She sat up, shoving his hands aside, whipping his belt off and tossing it...somewhere in the room. Her fingers deftly working at his fly, gliding it gently over his erection.

He sucked in a deep breath as she brought her mouth to him, taking as much as she could while she slid his pants to the floor.

She looked up at him as she lapped at the tip. "You like that, don't you?"

"You're still a dirty, nerdy girl."

She cupped him, squeezing as her thumb fanned the base of his cock, and her hot mouth nearly swallowed him whole.

He fisted her hair, watching her move over him, her hands following her mouth, doing his best to maintain some control. "Jesus Christ," he whispered. His pulse roared in his ears, and his chest heaved up and down. He pressed one hand against her cheek, feeling himself inside her hot mouth. "Stop," he commanded, but she sucked him harder and faster. His leg muscles tightened, and his skin erupted like hot lava.

He twisted her hair, tightening his grip, giving her a good tug.

"No," she said as her mouth slid off him. "I'm not done yet."

He pushed her mouth to him, gliding inside slowly, letting her have her fill. He couldn't remember the last time he'd been this hard.

Or this excited.

Her hands roamed his thighs and ass while she continued to take him to new heights of pleasure. Her fiery lips slid over his sensitive skin, and he could feel his pulse inside her hot mouth. She looked up at him with Heat-laden eyes.

He yanked her head off him with more force than intended, but she didn't seem to mind as she licked her lips.

"We better turn the TV on because you are not going to be able to be quiet, and I'm not covering your mouth."

She twisted her body, grabbing something from the nightstand and pointing in the direction of the television. Immediately, more light flickered against the curve of her sweet ass. He had no idea what show was on, or who was talking...nor did he care. He dropped to his knees, grabbing her by the legs, and spreading her wide.

"You're so fucking gorgeous."

She cupped his face. "Look up here, sailor, and say that again."

He laughed, pressing his finger on her swollen nub. "I'm not a sailor, and you call me that again and I won't do this." He slipped two fingers inside her. "Or this." He bent over, licking her. She tasted like coconut milk, and her moans sent his blood boiling.

Her fingers massaged his scalp, coaxing him deeper inside her. "Yes...Logan..." Her words were more like deep breaths. She grabbed his free hand, bringing it to her hard nipple. "God...yes."

He pinched and twisted while she wiggled against his mouth and fingers as he refused to go too deep or too intense. He wanted to tease her. Bring her close, but not over the edge. He wanted her to beg him to make her cum. Pulling his head back, he watched his fingers disappear inside her before he slid them out, inserting a third...then fourth finger. She grinded her hips against his hand desperately.

"Please...Logan...oh...God..." She ran her fingers through his hair, pushing him toward her. He smiled, knowing the moment he darted his tongue out and licked her, she'd convulse, spilling her orgasm over his fingers.

And she didn't disappoint him as he took her

swollen nub in his mouth and sucked hard while he rammed his fingers deep inside. Her body rocked and quivered as she pushed his head away, clasping her legs together, showing off those damned fuck-me pumps laced to her feet while she cried out his name.

He kissed her ankles as he slowly removed her shoes. "I have a crazy question."

"Yeah, what's that?" she asked in a throaty pant.

"Do you have a condom? Because if you don't, we're both going to be very disappointed."

She rolled away, leaping off the bed. The perspiration beading on her sexually drenched body glimmered in the moonlight.

He lay down and watched her walk across the room as her hips swayed and her bare ass caught the light from the bathroom in a perfect silhouette. "Are you really going to leave me hanging here?"

She laughed. "I stole a condom from my brother this morning."

"I think that's kind of gross and hot at the same time."

She disappeared, only to return and lean against the doorjamb, her hip jaunting away from the frame with a small package in her hand. Her naked body drenched with sex. "I only took one because I wasn't sure you'd ever take me up on my offer."

"I'm going to hell, *and* I'm going to lose my job." He adjusted himself to the middle of her bed. "Get your ass over here. I intend to make you cum again."

"You better." She climbed onto the bed, then ripped open the condom, rolling it over him while he hissed and cussed. Her fingers glided over his balls before she straddled him, taking all of him inside her in one slow luxurious stroke.

"You're so hot." He gripped her hips, grinding her against him in a slow but rhythmic motion.

Her hands pressed against his chest as she rode him, keeping things methodical until he rose up and sucked one of her nipples inside his mouth, grazing it with his teeth. His hand reaching between them, fingers rubbing her swollen nub.

"Oh...God. Logan...yes..."

"Oh yes, baby," he whispered against her breast, his fingers rubbing her in a hard circular motion until she squeezed around the length of him, her body quivering and jolting on top of him.

"That's it, baby," he said. "Say my name."

"Logan...oh...Logan." She jerked again. "Logan!"

He flipped her on her back, ramming himself deep inside her over and over again, her insides tightening around him. He buried his face in her neck. A guttural groan echoed across the room. He slammed himself one last time before letting his full weight fall on top of her.

She welcomed him by wrapping her legs around his waist, and they grinded slowly against one another until their breathing had returned to something that could be considered normal.

Logan rolled off, keeping her close and her head tucked neatly under his arm and against his chest.

"I think we have a problem," he whispered.

"What's that?"

"It's not out of my system, and we just might have to that again in the near future."

"I won't say no."

He laughed. His fingers slowly glided up and down her back, her arms and legs draped over his body. The scent of sex filled the room.

Letting his eyelids drop, he relaxed into her king-size bed, allowing himself a few minutes of shut-eye before he relieved his brother from guard duty. Twenty minutes later, he reluctantly slipped from Mia's bed, covering up her naked body with her soft sheets. He hiked up his jeans and looked for his shirt, which he thought he'd tossed near the closet, but it was nowhere to be found.

His phone buzzed, and Dylan's number flashed across the screen.

"What's up," Logan whispered, still searching for his T-shirt.

"We've got company."

Logan stiffened his back. "What kind of company?"

"I don't think it's the friendly kind," Dylan said. "There is a car parked down the road, and right now I'm watching a guy wearing all black walking around the Intracoastal side of the fence between the south side of the pool and the outdoor grill area."

"I'm on my way." Logan gave up on his shirt and belt as he quickly left Mia's bedroom, racing down the long hallway, only stopping to get his weapon.

Once outside, he eyed Dylan, who sat on top of the pool house and pointed, then made a climbing gesture.

Logan looked up at the tall tree with low swinging branches. He looked over his shoulder, checking the angle of the camera.

Not wanting whoever this person was to make it onto the Vanderlin property, Logan signaled his brother, then took off running. If he'd put his shoes on, he might have been able to do the run in less than three minutes, but since that wasn't the case, he just hoped he didn't step on anything that might cause bodily harm.

By the time he rounded the corner, the person climbing the tree had dropped to the ground outside the fence and took off toward the road.

Slowing for a second, Logan looked to the roof of the pool house where his brother made a motion, indicating the intruder had tossed something into the yard. His heart pounded, and his lungs burned as he picked up the pace, hauling ass, but whoever he chased seemed to be a world-class sprinter as he heard the roar of an engine.

By the time his feet hit the main road, the car disappeared in the night.

"Fuck," he muttered as jogged back to the main house where he met his brother near the pool area. "Please tell me you got a plate number?"

"I did." Dylan nodded. "Already have one of Nick's buddies running it."

"So, what did the asshole toss over the fence?"

Dylan pointed to a manila legal-sized envelope. "Interesting way to send mail."

"It's addressed to Mia." Logan knelt, carefully lifting the envelope by the corners. "Let's open it and see what we've got." The package weighed next to nothing. He wasn't sure if that was a good thing...or a bad thing.

He set it down on the picnic table near the pool

where dim lights helped him see better. He twisted the metal tabs and pulled back the unsealed flap before giving it a little shake. A piece of paper slipped out. "That's weird." He sat down, his brother looking over his shoulder, and read the words on the page.

*Mia,*

*This will appear in all major newspapers across the country in the next couple of days. Every news channel will pick up the story. This is what happens when you're so arrogant you get sloppy.*

*Is Mia Vanderlin a fraud, a criminal, AND a traitor?*

*An independent cyber company recently looked into the allegations that DANA Corp had been hacked by an underground organization called STEALTH while Miss Vanderlin was doing a cyber security check. However, the new company, which at this time would like to remain anonymous, uncovered that Mia not only fabricated the attack, making it look like STEALTH, but also stole top-secret information, which is still missing at this time. The CIA is looking into the new information provided by the independent company as well as questioning a group of hackers claiming they worked for Mia and her brother.*

*Raisin was here...*

"Who is Raisin?" Dylan asked.

"A motherfucker who is going to wish they hadn't fucked with my girlfriend."

# Chapter Nine

Mia stared into her mug of coffee, the steam floating into the air. She inhaled sharply, taking in the bitter smell mixed with a dash of fresh almonds. Her father sat directly across from her, and Logan leaned against the kitchen sink.

"I feel better that we're not dealing with STEALTH." Logan pulled out the chair at the end of the table and sat down.

"I honestly don't see how that's any better," her father said.

Logan sipped his coffee. "With that organization, there were so many other factors, including a very real possibility of physical harm."

"You don't know that this Raisin or whoever

doesn't want to hurt my baby girl." Her father leaned back in his chair and glared at Logan.

"You're right. I don't. That said, we're dealing with a very different beast with different motivations, and it seems Raisin is out to destroy Mia's reputation and—"

"A different kind of bodily harm." She shivered, sloshing some of her coffee on her hands. "I did move information to a server outside DANA Corp, which could be considered a federal crime, landing my ass in prison."

Logan reached across the table and took her hand. "I'm not going to let that happen."

"You're awfully sure of yourself, son." Her father leaned forward, pressing his hands on the table.

Logan continued to hold her hand, and either her father was oblivious, or he choose to ignore it. She doubted the latter.

"I've spent the last six years in Special Forces. All the people I work with today are ex-Special Forces, or military, former cops, or CIA and FBI agents. We know some interesting people in high places, and I'm calling in every favor I've got. I'm going to do what I was trained to do and that's find the threat and eliminate it."

She shivered again, and he squeezed her hand.

"But you can't guarantee anything, can you?"

"I can guarantee I will die trying."

Her father cracked a smile as he stood. "That, I believe." Her father turned and left the kitchen.

Logan dropped his head to the table with a thud. "Even after our talk yesterday, he still terrifies me."

"What kind of talk?" She ran her hand up and down his strong muscled back.

"A weird one where he liked me." He sat up, still holding her hand.

"He does like you." She smiled as warmth spread across her body. "My mom said he called the Aegis Network, knowing you worked there and specifically asked for you."

"Seriously?" Logan arched a brow.

She nodded.

*Buzzzzzzz.*

"It's Nick," Logan said, tapping his phone and putting it on speaker.

"Whatcha got for me?"

"The car that was at the house last night is registered to an Oscar Hiller."

"Does that sound familiar?" Logan asked Mia.

She glanced toward the ceiling, rolling the name around in her brain. "I don't think so, but maybe Markus knows him."

"Not necessary to ask," Nick said. "Dylan graduated with him, and guess who he's dating?"

"Bonnie," Logan said, leaning back in his chair. "Where is she now?"

"At the office. Dylan is watching. He'll let you know if she's on the move. I've got the boyfriend."

Mia's mind raced with a million possibilities. By the way Logan eyed her, he was going down the same rabbit hole.

"Any news on finding Rock or his ex?" he asked.

"Not yet," Nick said.

"I'll find Rock." For the first time since this shitstorm began, Mia's fingers itched to touch a keyboard.

"How are you going to do that?" Logan asked.

"If William Rockmann is indeed Raisin, then I'm calling him out, publicly. If not, the real Raisin is going to show his ugly head." She tucked her hair behind her ears, wishing she had a ponytail holder.

"I'm not sure I want you firing up your system." Logan tilted his head, rubbing his scruffy face. "Why don't we have Markus—"

"I'm going to need his help." Mia squirmed in her seat like a kid, her mind flowing like a set of perfectly running code, in search of bits of data. "But the only way this is going to work is if I come out and play.”

“She’s right,” Nick’s voice echoed through the air.

“All right. Talk soon.” Logan tapped the phone, ending the call. “I want to know the entire plan, how you and Markus are doing this, and I want my IT person involved.”

“Agreed.” She smiled. “We’re going to get this bastard.”

“Logan Michael Sarich,” his mother yelled.

He closed his eyes. “Those three words are worse than your father’s deadly stares,” he whispered. “In the kitchen!”

“For a macho guy, you’re kind of girly.” He’d always been a bit of an oxymoron, with his tough alpha exterior, but inside he was sweet and kind and sometimes reminded her of an innocent little boy.

He growled just as his mother stormed into the kitchen holding a belt and a white T-shirt.

“Oh, hi, Mia,” his mother said.

Heat exploded from her belly and rose to her cheeks. She wanted to crawl under the table. “Hi, Mrs. Sarich,” she said, trying to hide behind her coffee.

"Hi, Mom," Logan said, pointing his finger at the shirt. "Thanks?"

"Good grief. You two are grown adults." His mother slammed his clothing on the table. "But seriously, do you have no understanding of being discreet?"

"She did tell you that you didn't have to clean—"

"Don't go there, Logan Michael." His mother turned on her heels and stormed off much the same way she came in.

"So, was I worth it?" Mia rubbed her foot against his calf.

"Hell yeah."

"Then kiss me a proper good morning so I can get to work and catch Rock, Raisin, or whoever the fuck has been messing with me."

"I love it when you talk dirty."

"Stop talking and start kissing."

"I must have a death wish." He pushed back his chair, yanking her from hers and into his arms.

Her body pressed against his hard chest. Her nipples tingled, and her body ached. She licked her lips in anticipation.

"I don't think I will ever be able to get you out of my system," he whispered before his lips brushed against hers.

She moaned, closing her eyes, wanting more and more. His tongue swirled her mouth with as much power as his arms lifted her toes from the ground. Resisting the urge to lift her legs around his hard body, she patted his shoulder. "When this is over, we need to talk."

"You just told me to shut up." He squeezed her bottom and winked before his face turned serious. "What have you done to me, Mia Vanderlin?"

# Chapter Ten

"Are you sure you want to go in there with me?" Logan pointed to his mother's office building, staring at Dylan. "I imagine you don't want to see her ever again."

Dylan laughed. "That was a long time ago, and I've seen her a few times since then. Water under the bridge."

"I want to tell Mom so she'll fire the little hussy."

"I'm the one who took the pictures of my hard-on and sent it to her. It's called sexting. You should try it sometime."

Logan paused, turning his head. "Please don't tell me you still do that shit, cuz it will get you a boatload—"

"Relax." Dylan slapped Logan on the back. "I

understand the word 'discretion' unlike someone else I know who leaves their clothes behind." Dylan flashed a grin.

"How'd you know that?" Logan picked up the pace.

"Mom called and wanted to know what I knew. While she acted all embarrassed, secretly she's got you and Mia with a baby carriage."

Logan waited for the frustration to bubble to the surface. He understood why his mother wanted marriage and babies for her boys. Logan wasn't opposed to either, but he'd have to be in love and that concept had eluded him. He stopped dead in his tracks, scratching the back of his head.

*Mia. Love. No. Maybe?*

"What's wrong?" Dylan asked.

"Nothing." Logan's pulse skyrocketed. A thin layer of sweat beaded across the palms of his hands like it had done the first time he'd kissed Mia on their very first date at the Lighthouse.

*I'm in love with Mia.*

The corners of his mouth tipped upward. "Huh."

"What?" Dylan questioned.

Logan drew his hand over his mouth, wiping the grin off his face. "Let's go see what Bonnie really knows." He ignored his little brother's puzzled expression and marched forward, the restlessness he'd felt his entire life evaporated and had been replaced with the exhilaration he'd been chasing since he could remember.

Pulling open the door, Logan regained his focus. He had a job to do. "Hello, Bonnie," he said.

The redhead jumped in her seat, tossing her textbook to the ground. "Jesus, you scared me."

"Sorry." The front door closed, and Dylan leaned against it. "How ya doing?"

"Fine," Bonnie huffed out. "What do you want?"

"We have some questions for you." Logan sat on the edge of the desk.

She pushed her chair back, folding her hands across her chest. "I don't think your mother would appreciate you harassing her employees."

"I can send a cop over." Logan continued to stare at Bonnie. "Once they are done questioning your boyfriend."

Bonnie's eyes narrowed to tiny slits. "Why would the police want anything from Oscar?"

"Maybe you could tell us why he was at the Vanderlin home last night?" Logan shifted his gaze to the desk, looking at her notebook.

"He wasn't there." Her eyes stayed tiny slivers as she drew her lips tight.

"Yeah, he was," Dylan said, pushing himself from the door. "What I don't understand is what do you or Oscar know about STEALTH? I mean, you didn't get the computer geek gene like your brother, and Oscar was more into smoking weed than school."

"I have no idea what you're talking about, now leave." She pointed to the front door with a shaky finger.

"Not until you tell us how you're involved with whoever is threatening Mia Vanderlin," Logan said, leaning forward, noticing a few blonde strands peeking out from the bottom drawer.

Bonnie pushed the chair back until it hit the wall. "I'm going to call the police," her voice trembled.

"Be my guest." Dylan inched forward, but Logan stopped him.

No need to scare her even more.

"Look." Logan ran a hand over his head. "We can do this the easy way, or the hard way."

"Are you threatening me?" she shrieked.

Logan shook his head. "The hard way is we call the cops." He opened the bottom drawer and pulled out a wig, holding it up. "The girl you hired to follow Mia will be able to ID you. We know you gave her a key and asked her to call you, so you would have a record of the call."

"But I bet that was your brother's idea." Dylan tilted his head. "Cuz you're not that smart."

"Fuck you," Bonnie said. "I'm not telling you jack shit."

"It will go better for you if you tell us where Raisin and Theresa are." Logan watched as Bonnie's eyes went wide, then narrowed again, confirming in his mind that Raisin was indeed Rock and the mastermind behind the entire attack on Mia. "What you've done is minor compared to them, so I'm sure the cops will cut you a deal."

"I don't know where he is," she said. Her arms folded tight as she lowered her gaze. "I haven't seen him since right before he dropped out of college."

"Are you serious?" Dylan asked, standing next to Logan. "How did he contact you then?"

"He hacked me a year ago, and he's been making me do this shit for him."

Dylan laughed. "Yeah, right. And I've got a Lighthouse for sale."

"You're such an asshole." She raised her gaze. "Rock has control of my bank accounts, all my social media; he even changed a grade in one of my graduate courses, fucking with my GPA. He did the same thing to Oscar."

"That sucks." Logan dropped the wig on the desk. "I'm only going to ask this question once. If you say no, I won't help you with the cops."

"What do you want?" She dropped her hands to her lap, relaxing her body.

"I want you to let Mia into your computer system, so she can flush out your brother, and we can put an end to this."

Bonnie bit down on her lower lip. "Will she help me get control of all my finances and personal online life? Oscar's too?"

"We'll make sure it happens." Logan pushed from the desk. "But you also have to tell us everything you know about his plan to destroy Mia."

"I don't know much, but I can tell you it's not going as he orchestrated, and he hadn't anticipated you showing up."

"All right then." Logan held out his hand. "Let's get with the local police so we do this right." Logan held Bonnie by her elbow as he guided her out of the office, making sure the door was locked before tucking her into Dylan's car.

"You good with dealing with her?" Logan asked as he made his way to the driver's side of his Jeep.

"I couldn't care less about her and haven't in years." Dylan waved. "It's not true what they say about your first."

"She was your first?"

Dylan shrugged. "We've all made mistakes."

"My first wasn't a mistake." Logan smiled. "I'm thinking about making my first, my last."

The shocked expression plastered on his little brother's face made it all the sweeter. Now all he had to do was eliminate the threat and then tell Mia's father that he planned on deflowering his daughter for the rest of his life.

# Chapter Eleven

Mia slipped off her headphones and rubbed her shoulder as she peered over the computer screen and stared at the sexy man she'd come to love. Or maybe her mother was right, and she'd loved him all along.

Logan leaned against the doorjamb to her bedroom. His muscles flexed under his T-shirt.

"How long have you been standing there?"

"Ten minutes," he said, pushing himself from the door and sauntering in her direction. "I didn't want to disturb or scare you."

"That is why I never have my back to the door." She craned her neck, trying to get the kinks out. "What time is it?"

"Close to midnight. Here. Let me help you with that." He stood behind her, his long fingers curling over her shoulders and neck as he found all the sore spots and worked magic on her muscles. "Feel good?"

"Oh...God...yes."

"That sounds familiar, but you left off my name."

"Logan...oh, Logan." She laughed, dropping her chin to her chest, letting him take away all the tension the last few hours had created. "Rock hasn't taken any bait I've sent. I'm not even sure he knows I want to play."

"I suspect he knows, but he's waiting for what he thinks is the right time."

"That's what scares me. He's deep underground as it is. He could disappear and in a year or two, come at me again. Seems that's his MO."

"I was thinking about that." He rolled her chair in front of her bed and sat down, still rubbing her shoulders. "When you mentioned calling him out publicly, I didn't understand you meant underground with a bunch of hackers, where it seems he's well protected. So, I was thinking we bring him out into the real world."

"What do you mean?"

He spun the chair around, holding the armrests.

His turquoise eyes staring deep into her soul. "We have the note Oliver tossed over the fence. We have Bonnie willing to do whatever it takes. STEALTH has said they had nothing to do with the hack."

"But we don't have any code from Raisin... Rock...in any of the files."

"Markus is still working on that, and I have faith he'll find it." Logan reached out and tucked a piece of hair that had fallen from her ponytail behind her ear. "Rock has always been jealous of you, and he's never liked you."

"Not true." Mia looked toward the window, leaning away from his touch, but Logan pressed his thumb under her chin, tilting her head.

"What do you mean by that?"

"We'd always been competitive with each other since middle school, but he wasn't vicious back then."

"He was with Markus," Logan said.

"That didn't start until eighth grade." She took in a deep breath, knowing this conversation could go sour quickly. "Right after I told him I wouldn't go to the movies with him. That I'd never go out with him, and when he tried to kiss me, I slapped him, in front of the entire science club."

"I see." Logan leaned back, dropping his hands to his lap. "I didn't know that."

"Not sure any of the popular kids or jocks would have cared to hear that juicy piece of nerd gossip."

Logan arched a brow. "You turned him down, and that's when he started messing with you, and he's held that grudge since you were fourteen?"

"For the next two years, he made my life miserable, so I thought if I went on one date with him and—"

"You seriously went out with him?" Logan's face contorted into something that looked like Play-Doh that had been squeezed by a toddler. He rubbed the back of his neck. "So, tell me what happened on the date."

"My goal had been to make him hate me, so I did everything I could to put him down. I even told him that his strategy in the science fair project sucked and that Markus was going to win. I'd be right after my brother and Rock wouldn't even place."

"He did say you were a conceited stuck-up bitch at prom, along with a few other things."

"So glad you didn't hit him that night."

"I'm not." Logan stood. "He said some weird things to me about you."

"I've always wondered what he might have said."

She rose and stood behind him, resting her hands on his hips. "I was so mean to him on that date I figured I was walking home, but he wanted to go to the movies, and I was like, Jesus, are you that blind to the fact you disgust me?"

"What happened at the movies?" Logan's body stiffened.

"He tried to push the wrong girl, and I kind of hurt him where it counts and ended up calling my dad to come get me."

Logan turned, wrapping his arms around her. "Did you tell your father what happened?"

"I didn't have a choice; my shirt was ripped."

Logan's eyes closed briefly. "Did Rock hurt you?"

"No," she said. "He got a little too touchy-grabby, and I put an end to it."

"Why didn't you ever tell me?"

"By the time we started dating, Rock had transferred schools. And I knew you well enough to know you'd haul off and hit him if I told you what happened, so there was that."

"Yeah, well, when I find that dried-up prune, I'm going to give him a long overdue fist through his teeth."

Mia smiled. "My dad did call the police. Your

father came, and I'm not exactly sure what went down, but Rock did stay clear of me after that."

"No, he didn't." Logan cupped her face. "He might have stayed away from you in this world, but he's been coming at you in the hacker world for over a decade, and I'm going to make sure the dipshit gets what he deserves." He kissed her nose. "Nobody messes with my woman and gets away with it."

She opened her mouth to question his words, but instead she raised up on tiptoe and crash-landed her lips to his in a wet entanglement of passion. His hot tongue met hers with a sense of hunger. Her arms wrapped tightly around his waist, fingers dug into his taut muscles. "Lock the door," she managed. "I'll get the condom."

He pulled away, his chest heaving up and down. "You stole another one?"

"I took the whole box."

He growled, ripping off his shirt.

"I love that noise. You make it when you orgasm, and you always have."

"How do you know I always do?"

"Always with me and that's all that matters."

He growled again, and every inch of her body sizzled. Grabbing the box off the dresser in her closet, she raced back to the bed where Logan had already stripped down to nothing, his glorious toned body glistening in the moonlight.

"Well, hello there." She tossed him the box before turning on the television, keeping the volume low, but high enough she wasn't worried about anyone hearing her and Logan. "We're crazy, you know that?" As she yanked her shirt over her head, his fingers fiddled with the front clasp of her bra.

"Our inability to keep our hands to ourselves certainly says something about us." He scooped her off the floor and laid her on her back, kissing her neck, cupping a breast in his protective hand.

"What exactly does it say?" She cupped his face, forcing him to look at her. She searched his eyes for something that told her he didn't feel the same way. Part of her wanted this to be a trip down memory lane.

Part of her wanted it to be forever.

He propped himself up on his side, his warm arm draped over her middle. His green eyes turned a softer shade of turquoise. "I don't know about you, but I don't want to walk away from you this time."

"I've thought about you over the years, hoping you never found anyone, but wishing you nothing but happiness."

"I'm happy right now."

She'd never been one to cry, but a single tear formed in the corner of her eye. "I didn't know how unhappy and unfulfilled I'd been until I saw you pull into our driveway the other day. It's crazy, but I'm pretty sure I lov—"

He hushed her with his forefinger. More tears welled in her eyes as insecurity rose from her toes to her brain. "Logan—"

"Shhhh," he whispered as he undid her pants, lowering them over her hips, kissing her belly button. "Let me show you how I feel."

Mia arched her back as his tongue glided across her intimately. Her pants and underwear pooled at her ankles while she desperately tried to kick them off. She caught his gaze. His fingers deep inside her, stroking her tenderly. Lovingly. Without the urgency of need, but laced with a deep abiding affection.

She gripped the sheets, staring down at him while he loved her in a way she'd never experienced. Sex with him had always been mind-blowing and wild. Raw and out of control. As young lovers, they couldn't keep their hands off each other, constantly exploring and experimenting. But now she found herself wanting something more than the physical orgasms. She wanted the emotional one too.

She watched as he wrapped the condom over

himself before settling between her legs, staring into her eyes. He pressed himself against her, easing in slowly.

She dug her heels into the mattress as she lifted her hips. He kept his hands pressed into the bed by her shoulders, lifting himself in and out of her in a single deliberate motion.

"Oh...Logan..." she whispered, turning her head and closing her eyes.

"Look at me," he said in a deep throaty groan. "Don't take your eyes off me."

She shifted, grinding against him.

"No," he whispered. His eyes changed into a kaleidoscope of green. "Move with me."

He continued to move his hips in a leisurely circular motion, nearly pulling all the way out before gliding back in, her nerve endings sparking like firecrackers. Her body matched his pace as she dug her fingernails into his back but resisted the urge to grab his ass while she wrapped her legs around him, forcing him to pound her harder and faster.

Her chest tightened as she stared into his eyes, mesmerized by the way he looked deep into her soul. Her chest heaved up and down. "Logan..." she panted, her eyelids drooping but never breaking their trance. She arched her back, rocking with him, becoming one with him. At that moment, she knew Logan Sarich belonged only to her, and he always had.

He smiled as if he knew exactly what she was thinking.

He leaned in and brushed his lips against hers, still looking deep into her eyes. The rolling of his hips came in quicker strokes as he raised his chest up, his arms stretched out. "Mia," he whispered. "Do you understand what you mean to me?"

She swallowed her breath.

He smiled. "Do you know how I feel about you?"

She opened her mouth to respond, but only a deep moan came out. Her body was on the verge of exploding. Her insides clutching him with force, feeling every inch of him in a way she'd never experienced.

"Tell me how I feel, Mia." He came down on his elbows, his hands holding the sides of her head.

"I lov—"

He hushed her with a quick kiss. "No. Tell *me* how *I* feel."

She blinked, her body confused between the desperate need to have release and the deep abiding love her soul needed to share. Her mind told her they were one and the same. The way he held her, rocked her, stared at her... "You love me."

His eyes rolled back as he slammed himself inside her.

"Oh, my God..." Her body quivered as if she'd been shocked with adrenaline mixed with a dose of raw primal need.

He growled, and her body exploded again.

"Oh...yes...Logan!"

He sucked on her earlobe as he continued to stroke, whispering her name until he let out a long breath and collapsed on top of her.

She roamed his back with her hands, massaging his neck and shoulders, occasionally grazing his spine with her fingernails.

"Was that just a way to get out of saying those three words?"

He laughed, rolling to his side, kissing her neck and her cheek before cupping her face. His eyes laden with something other than lust...something real...something permanent.

"I have no problem saying I love you, Mia Vanderlin, but I needed to know you felt how much I love you."

Her breath hitched as her body filled with the

warmth she'd been missing all her adult life. "That's more romantic than how you asked me to prom."

"I have my moments."

She took in a deep breath and let it out slowly. "I love you."

"I know."

She closed her eyes and snuggled into the crook of his shoulder. The sense of not knowing where she belonged dissipated into thin air.

# Chapter Twelve

Logan hiked up his jeans, securing the zipper and button. He glanced over at Mia, who sat behind him at her desk, headphones on, wearing a tank top and jean shorts. Doing whatever it was she did while listening to some heavy metal band that sounded more like a bunch of pigs being castrated than music.

The corners of his mouth tipped upward. He had no idea what the future held except that some-how, someway, Mia would be a part of it.

The night sky turned a pale shade of gray-blue as a new day approached. He glanced around the room, looking for his shirt. He wasn't going to sneak down-stairs without it this time.

Mia jumped, kicking back her chair. "I found

him!" She tried to yank her headphones off, but they tangled in her messy ponytail. "Crap." She fiddled with her hair, untangling the strands, and tossed the massive headphones on the desk, headbanging music still blaring. "We need to get Markus in here... No, we'll go to him."

"I need to find my damn shirt."

She unplugged her laptop. "Let's go; I don't want to lose him." She squeezed Logan's bare shoulder before racing across the room.

He continued to scan the floor when Mia pulled open her door and skidded to a stop.

"Morning, Dad," she said.

Logan put his hands on his hips and closed his eyes, heat rising to his cheeks. At least his pants were actually on this time.

"No time to chat, Dad. I've finally gotten that bastard Rock to come out and play."

Logan opened his eyes as Mia scooted around her father, who stood in the doorway, staring at Logan with narrowed yes. "Good morning, Mr. Vanderlin." Logan eyed his shirt under the bed and knelt, snagging the cotton fabric and pulling it over his head, hoping Mr. Vanderlin had left.

But nope. There he stood. Hands on his hips, still glaring.

"I need to go see what Markus and Mia are doing and figure out our next move so I can eliminate the threat," Logan said, sucking in a deep breath.

Mr. Vanderlin stepped to the side, holding his arm out.

Logan headed toward the door, contemplating if he should have a man to man talk now or later.

He opted for later.

"Logan." Mr. Vanderlin grabbed Logan's arm just as he was about to pass.

Guess this talk was going to happen now. "I don't know if this is going to make this situation less awkward or not, but I spent the last fourteen years of my life looking for the one thing that told me I was in the right place, doing the right thing. I never expected that I would find what I'd been searching for back here, but I did and—"

"Logan," Mr. Vanderlin said with an arched brow.

"Please, sir. Let me finish. I went off to college believing I would someday be a pitcher in the major leagues, and in the back of my mind I figured Mia would be at my side. When my father died, I lost it and pushed everything I loved away, including baseball...including Mia. I chased the adrenaline rush, which doesn't do anything but leave one dissatisfied after the rush is over. Being back here, with Mia, well, sir, it feels like home. I care a great deal for her, and I would never do anything to hurt her." Logan took in a deep breath and let it out slowly.

"Are you finished?"

"Yes, sir."

"Okay. First, cut the Mr. and sir crap. You're not seventeen anymore. Call me Brett."

"Yes, sir...Brett." Logan swallowed the lump in his throat.

"Second. That is all fine and dandy, but not necessary and not what I wanted to talk to you about." Brett placed a hand on Logan's back and started walking toward Markus' room.

"Oh," was all Logan could manage.

"I know you wouldn't do anything to intentionally hurt my daughter. But that asshole Rock did. I don't know if Mia or your father ever told you what happened."

"Mia told me." Logan clenched his fists. "Yesterday."

"Seeing my little girl with her shirt torn and bruises on her arm was a million times worse than catching her in bed with a decent young man who cared about her."

Logan stopped and faced Brett. "My father was called that night. Was Rock arrested?"

Brett nodded. "We filed charges, got a restraining order, and Rock had to go to another school, and I thought that had been the end of it. It wasn't until the state science fair her senior year that I found out he'd been tampering with her projects, but we couldn't prove anything, and he seemed to have disappeared after that."

"When we find that asshole, I'm going to bruise both his eyes."

"I wouldn't mind punching the weasel once. I tried to that night, but your father stopped me." Brett put his hand on Logan's shoulder. "Your father was a good man. We had drinks about a week after you went off to college. He was very grateful he never had a daughter." Brett let out a light laugh.

Logan cracked a smile but didn't dare make a noise.

"Logan!" Mia's voice echoed down the hallway. "Get in here!"

Logan took long strides, Mia's father right behind him.

"What is it?"

"You're not going to like it." Mia sat on Markus' bed, legs crisscrossed with her computer on her lap, staring up at him with determination glowing in her soft, caring eyes.

"He should be sitting down for this," Markus said, pounding away on his keyboard.

"Spill it." Logan planted his hands on his hips, holding her gaze.

She set her laptop aside, uncrossed her legs, and set her feet on the floor. "Rock says he has a proposition for me and wants to meet."

"Over my dead body," her father said.

"Like hell." Logan narrowed his eyes. "But I'll meet with him."

She shook her head. "That won't work. He wants me, and I think—"

"Well, stop thinking," Logan barked. "Because there is no way in hell I'm letting that asshole anywhere near you."

"Let me finish." Mia stood and closed the gap. "He says he'll put an end to destroying my career if I'll help him with something."

"He's not going to stop." Her father stood next to Markus' desk, peering over his son's shoulder, looking at all the screens. "And you know I'm right."

"We can make him stop." Mia rested her hands on Logan's shoulders.

"Bingo!" Markus pushed his chair back and

swiveled in a complete 360. "Rock is STEALTH, which is why STEALTH denied the hack."

"Fuck," Logan muttered. "All the more reason you're not meeting with Rock."

She shook her head. "I have to meet with him. It's the only way we can nail the bastard. We pull him off his system, away from the only world he knows and understands, and we can not only bust him for the DANA Corp hack, but we can bust up his entire operation."

"No." Logan shrugged her hands off his shoulders and started to pace. "You are *not* meeting him. End of discussion. I'll call my boss and get our IT girl on all this."

"She's already in on it," Markus said. "Everything we do, Misky sees."

"Good, but I'm still not using Mia as bait. The members of STEALTH are dangerous and not just in cyberspace."

"I'm with Logan on this one." Her father leaned against the back wall. "Can't you work behind the scenes? Meet with him in cyberspace or something?"

"That's what he wants," Mia said.

Logan scratched the back of his neck. "That, I'd let happen."

"Don't you get it? He'd only be distracting me so

that he can get back into this system and find where I parked those files."

"That's what he wants help with?"

"I suspect that's part of it, but based on what is in those files, I'm going to wager he wants me to hack into the Department of Defense and find military tactical plans for specific locations relating to what DANA Corp is doing."

"But the CIA has those files." Logan stopped and stared at her.

"They do, but I had to shut down before I wiped the server of all traces of those files, and the moment I logged in last night, Markus has been shifting things around, keeping Rock from hacking in again, but it won't last. If I meet with him in the cyber world, he'll get those files, and he'll destroy me."

Logan rubbed his neck, letting her words sink into his brain. "You're saying he's better than the two of you combined."

"He's not," Markus said, peering over the screen. "But he's got a top-notch team, and we can't keep up with them. Not even with Misky's help, and we don't have enough time to assemble a team we trust. But if we force him out to where he's not communicating with his team for a long enough time frame, Misky and I can get in, get what we need, then you or whoever can arrest him."

"After I hit him," Logan said under his breath. "Do we know where Rock is?"

"He's somewhere in South Florida, but we don't have an exact location," Markus said.

He turned to face Mia. "Have you asked to meet him in person?"

She shook her head. "I wanted to talk it over with you. Figured we'd need to formulate a plan before I did that, and we also have to make sure Markus and Misky have my back while I go into cyberland."

Logan let out a long breath. "Get him to agree to meet you, but I pick the location, and I'll need enough time to call in a few more favors because no way are you going in without at least a dozen sniper rifles aimed at Rock's ugly-ass head."

# Chapter Thirteen

*T**he following evening...***

Logan adjusted his earpiece.

"We've got hostiles," Dylan's voice crackled over the radio. "Two SUVs parked a half-mile down the road. Engines running."

"Fuck," Logan muttered. "Where the hell is Ramey? He was supposed to be here twenty minutes ago." Number three brother would be late for his damn funeral.

"For fuck's sake," Ramey's voice echoed. "Relax. I ran into some bad weather on the flight over here. It does take a while to fly from Vegas to Florida, just saying."

"Where are you?"

"At the house with my buddies. We're getting into place now."

Logan gripped the weapon in his lap as he raced across the bridge, listening to Mia order a drink. "You have to leave Markus alone, but keep an eye on him. I couldn't risk moving his computers or take him off STEALTH's tail."

"He's still one weird dude," Ramey said.

"Nick?" Logan questioned.

"Mr. and Mrs. Vanderlin are tucked away at a hotel, under the watchful eye of one of Jupiter's finest," Nick said.

"You're sure Rock is headed this way?" Ramey questioned.

"I've got a man up in the Lighthouse with eyes on him now. He's sitting in a boat, waiting for Mia. If our intel is correct, he plans on using Mia's or her brother's system to hack into the Department of Defense." Logan slammed on the brakes as he skidded into the marina.

"You're really going to let him and his goons walk into the Vanderlin home?" Ramey asked. "Putting Markus at risk."

"Markus knows exactly what we're doing. He's the one who helped dig up the intel." Logan snagged his duffel bag from the back of his Jeep.

"I can't believe Mia went for this plan," Nick said.

"She doesn't know all the details."

All three of his brothers, along with the rest of the team he'd assembled, muttered various superlatives.

"Shut up, all of you," Logan growled. "She's not stupid, and she'll figure it out when I don't stop her from getting on that boat. I prepared her for various scenarios."

"You are so sleeping in the doghouse tonight, big brother." Dylan laughed.

"Screw you." Logan tossed his bag into the small single engine pleasure boat. "At least I have a woman to put me in the doghouse."

"Ramey," Dylan said. "Make sure your men are in place, the SUVs are on the roll."

"On it," Ramey replied.

"Let's shut the chatter down unless necessary. Watch your backs." Logan jumped into the boat and focused on the sound coming from Mia's wire.

*I've got your back, baby.*

Mia sat at an outside table at one of the restaurants on the Jupiter Inlet directly across from the Lighthouse. Red, orange, and purple streaks lined the sky as the sun set over the bridge. She sipped her club soda that she'd gotten at the bar, looking around for Rock, trying to look casual. She wished she had one of those wire things jammed into her ear so she could hear the cool timbre of Logan's voice.

One of the waitresses working the outside tables rushed down the stairs toward her.

"Are you Mia?" the waitress asked.

She nodded.

"This is for you." The waitress handed her an envelope. "Can I get you anything else while I'm here?"

"No, thanks." Mia tensed her arm, making sure her hands didn't shake as she took the small white envelope. "Who is this from?"

"I don't know," the waitress admitted as she looked around. "The hostess asked me to bring it to you."

"I see."

The waitress shrugged, then turned and scurried off to another table.

Mia fiddled with the flap, waiting for a sign she shouldn't open it, but that didn't happen. She tore off the front flap and pulled out a piece of paper. She decided that whispering the note with tight lips would be a good idea.

"Mia, go to the last dock and walk to the end. There is a small boat waiting for you. If you don't, not only will I ruin you, but I'll put a hit on Logan, and trust me when I tell you I've got an army of ex-military on my payroll. Raisin was here."

Her hands trembled. She scrunched the paper and fisted her hands. Motherfucker wasn't going to mess with her or anyone she loved anymore. She chugged her club soda and slammed the empty plastic cup on the table. As she stood, she rolled her head, contemplating putting in her earbuds and blasting Guns N' Roses. It would be the only thing that could possibly reduce the speed at which her heart hammered in her chest. Pure adrenaline, she could handle. But not a pulse raging out of control.

The salty air mixed with the tacky humidity clung to her like honey on a spoon. She counted five pelicans perched on tall posts as she slowly walked down the far dock, putting new meaning to 'walk the plank.' She spied a mini-sized pontoon boat parked at the end. One man sat behind the center console. He looked her way and waved.

She put a hand over her eyes, blocking the setting sun, but still couldn't get a look at the man. At least she assumed it was a man.

By the time she got to the end of the dock, she figured Logan was peachy keen with her getting in this boat.

"Mia Vanderlin?" A familiar voice smashed into her ears, causing her to shiver.

"Rock," she spat out the single word. She stepped onto the bow of the boat, still unable to get a clear view of his face as he'd turned sideways to push the boat from the dock.

He wore a Marlin's baseball cap. His long wavy brown hair flowed over his shoulders. He was broader than she remembered, and his taste in clothing had gone off the rails with his orange pine tree shirt and blue cotton shorts. It hurt her eyes just looking at him. Not wanting her back to the asshole, she sat on the front side seat where she could see him and where they were headed.

"You look well," Rock said. He pushed down on the throttle and maneuvered the boat down the inlet and toward the ocean. A breeze kicked up, but it didn't cool her down. It just reminded her how much she'd been perspiring as her shirt gripped her body.

"Cut the small talk and let's get down to business."

He laughed. "Your feistiness has always been such a turn on."

She rolled her eyes. "Seriously. I don't have time to play any more games. What do you want from me?"

"I want a lot of things. But let's start with access to the real files you stole from me."

"I didn't steal them from you; I simply prevented you from having them."

"Now who's playing games." He turned the boat toward Indian River, also known as Jupiter Sound.

She swallowed. Logan had mentioned many possibilities regarding her meeting with Rock, but not one of them mentioned returning to her family home. At least not tonight.

"What else?" she asked, casually leaning back in the seat, draping both arms over the railing as if she were enjoying an evening on the water. To keep her body from trembling, she focused on the hum of the engine and the voices echoing across the water. It wasn't headbanging music by any means, but it helped.

"You're going to hack into the Department of Defense and get me their tactical plans for a nuclear threat on American soil. Specifically, the specs on the HOOVER-PIN and where it's located."

"What's that?"

"Don't play dumb with me. It's not attractive on you."

"If I do this and that's a big if." She tried not to scan other boats, hoping to see Logan or one of his brothers. "I'll have only ten minutes to get in and out before they have a lock on my IP, even routing it through five different third world countries."

"I'd say we have closer to twenty with you, me, and your brother working on it."

She let out a long sigh. "Who, then, is responsible for the hack, because I'm not doing it if you're just going to take me and Markus down. The only reason I'm meeting with you is to be able to clear my name."

Rock laughed that god-awful snorting laugh. Talk about unattractive. "STEALTH will take credit, but you and Markus are going to have to make sure I'm protected."

"But you are STEALTH." She blinked, trying to mute his stupid laugh.

"No one knows that, and you're going to make

sure it stays that way. You get me what I want and protect me, and I will make sure the allegations of you stealing from DANA Corp go away and Logan gets to live."

"You can't touch him."

She noted they were only a mile from her childhood home. A mile from where either shit was going to go right, or very, very, very wrong.

"My organization goes deep and dangerous. Don't underestimate me."

*Don't underestimate Logan and his brothers.*

*Or me.*

"The only way I'll do it is if you have STEALTH take credit and prove they did the hack on DANA Corp. That I was collateral damage. Then, and only then, will I hack the Department of Defense."

"Deal," Rock said.

In her mind, he said that a little too quickly, but what did it matter? He wasn't going to follow through with his end of the bargain, and neither was she. The only issue now was if her brother and Misky had enough time to get the Department of Defense to agree to their plan and whether or not Rock believed she'd do what he asked.

He pulled out his phone and tapped on the screen before putting it to his ear. "Clear Mia," he said, then set the phone on the console. "You'll be getting notification before we hit your dock that STEALTH is responsible for DANA Corp. Formalities of you being cleared will take place in the morning. I promise."

*Yeah, right.* She trusted him about as far as she could toss a baseball, and she couldn't even get it from the pitcher's mound over home plate.

"Thank you," she said, bile smacking the back of her throat. In the distance, she could see the dock with the family yacht tucked neatly between two piers. The lights from the property illuminated the sky.

*Let the hacking games begin.*

***

Logan watched as Mia walked gracefully down the dock toward the main house where she disappeared behind tall, lush trees with Rock, the asshole, by her side.

"Mia's entering the house," he whispered as he pulled up to the dock, hiding the small boat behind the forty-foot yacht. "What do we have inside?"

"Total of eight men," Ramey said. "One at the front door. One at the side patio door. One at the kitchen door and one near the pool house. I don't have eyes on the inside."

"I do," Dylan said. "Two men parked outside of Markus' room. One at the bottom of the spiral staircase and one standing guard in front of Mia's room."

"I'm a little scared you know the intimate details of my girlfriend's house." Logan secured his boat before opening up his duffel bag, snagging a few smoke bombs, a grenade, and two military grade pistols.

"So, it's official," Ramey said. "You're a kept man."

Logan shook his head, refusing to comment as he untied the pontoon boat, pushing it from the dock and letting the current take it down the river. If things went bad, he didn't want Rock to be able to escape by sea. "Once Mia is in Markus' room and in front of the computer, start systematically taking out the threat. I've got the one at Mia's door."

"You really going to climb the lattice?" Nick said. "You're getting too old for that shit."

"Time to clear the radio of any unnecessary chatter." Logan tucked one gun in his belt while checking the other was fully loaded and ready to go. He ran to the side of the pool house, watching Ramey deal with one of Rock's men, rendering him unconscious. He then secured his hands with Safariland restraints.

Ramey pointed to the kitchen door, then raced across the yard, nailing the second guy in the back of the head with the butt of his gun, and securing him as well.

"Front door dealt with," Ramey said.

"Back door secure," one of Ramey's men said.

Logan's cue to climb the lattice. He checked his watch. Ten minutes since Mia entered the house. Ten more minutes before the hack would be 'officially' detected by the Department of Defense, though Logan wasn't entirely sure what Misky, Asher, and Decker had worked out with the government regarding this op, and it didn't matter. All he needed to do was focus on making sure Mia and Markus were safe, and Rock and his gang of misfits were taken into custody.

He stared at the white lattice that lined the side of the house. Fourteen years ago, the wood makeshift ladder was unstable at best. He worried then, it would crumble under his weight, and he was a good fifteen pounds lighter back then. Grabbing ahold of the lattice, he gave it a good shake. It didn't move much, which was a good sign. He eased his foot into one of the holes and hoisted himself up, climbing quickly but carefully.

When his feet hit Mia's patio, he let out a long breath and retrieved his weapon. Slinking against the side of the house, keeping his pulse in check by methodical breathing and sheer power of will, he scanned the room. Light filtered in through the open door to the hallway. A long shadow covered the floor. He laced his fingers around the sliding glass door handle and pulled it back without making a sound.

"Perimeter of the house is clear," Ramey said.

"Downstairs is clear," Dylan said. "Ready for the distraction?"

"It's a go." Just as the word 'go' came out of Logan's mouth, the crackle of breaking glass echoed through the house.

Two men, one from in front Markus' room and the one guarding Mia's, ran down the hallway.

"Where are you, Nick?"

"The master bedroom. Once you step into the hallway, you'll be seen, but I've got your back."

Logan sucked in a deep breath, letting it out slowly. "On three... One, two, three..." He stepped into the hallway, weapon stretched out in front. The man guarding Markus' door lifted his assault rifle. Nothing like being outgunned.

"I wouldn't do that if I were you." Logan continued to move down the hallway. His heart beating a little faster. Out of the corner of his eye, he saw Nick's shadow.

"Boss, we've got company," the man said.

"I suspected we might." Rock appeared in the doorway, holding a computer. "You were so busy trying to protect the Vanderlins that you neglected your own loved ones." He tilted the screen, showing Logan's mother, sitting in her home, watching television...

"You piece of shit," Logan muttered.

"I've got a sniper just outside your mom's house. Anything happens to me, she's..." Rock held his finger to his head and twitched his thumb. "Bang, dead."

Logan moved his weapon, pointing it directly at Rock's head. "Get your man off my mother." He swallowed.

Nick's shadow slinked back into the master bedroom.

Rock laughed. "Put your gun down. My man can hear me, so all I have to do is give the order."

Logan loosened his grip on his weapon and held it up. "You touch my mother, and I will fucking kill you with my bare hands."

"I'm certain you didn't come alone so tell your gang to stand down." Rock took Logan's gun. "And to let my men go."

"Dylan," Ramey said over the wire. "You take care of Mom. My men and I will take care of this."

"Stand down," Logan said. "Let Rock's men go." He knew damn well his brothers weren't going to do that, and if his sense of time was correct, they had only a few minutes before Rock realizes Mia didn't hack the Department of Defense at all.

"Rock doesn't know his men personally," Ramey said. "All contracted, so my men are taking their place."

"You can't be sure," Nick whispered.

Logan couldn't stand to listen to the chatter any longer, so he took his earpiece out as he entered Markus' room. Mia and her brother sat next to each other, headphones on, staring at computer screens. They both glanced up and acknowledged Logan's presence, but that was about it.

"My team is standing down, now call your guy off my mother."

Rock shook his head, setting the laptop down, Logan's mother still on the screen. "Not until this is over and me and my men walk out of here." He glanced at his wrist where he sported an Apple

Watch. "Which should be done in less than ten minutes."

Logan squeezed his fists. When this was over, he and Rock were going one round, because that was all it was going to take for Logan to knock the asshole senseless.

"We've got a problem." Mia shoved her headphones to the side. "There is a second key code to unlock HOOVER-PIN."

"How did you not know that?" Rock motioned to his man to keep a gun on Logan while he stood behind Mia.

"They change the entry point randomly every five hours, and it's like the nuclear codes. We got into the first one, but if we hit the wrong key, we're locked out, and choppers will be over my house in less than five minutes."

"Find a way in and do it fast, or your boyfriend and his mother will take one for the team."

Logan eyed Mia, wondering what the hell she was up to.

"You're going to have to help me," Mia said, shoving her chair over, making room for Rock. "I need you to reroute a potential threat, then Markus and I can worm our way in."

Rock let out an exasperated sigh as he set the gun

down. "Can't fucking believe you won that scholarship over me."

Logan took the opportunity in the shift of focus from him to the hacking problem and scanned the room. Rock's goon stood at the door, rifle in hand, aimed at Logan.

Not good.

Rock put the weapon on the desk, just a half-foot from reach.

Not as bad as it could be.

"Hey, you came to me for help," Mia said.

Logan glanced over his shoulder, and she cracked a smile.

He arched a brow.

Rock sat behind the desk, folding open another laptop. "That's funny, because I recall it was you who begged to meet with me and clear your name."

Whatever Mia had up her sleeve, Logan was just going to have to run with it. He turned his attention back to the man with the rifle.

Nick's shadow eased across the floor, his fingers doing a whirly, finishing up with go, go, go, sign.

*Go the fuck where?*

"What the fuck!?" Rock stood, slamming his chair against the wall.

Logan spun around.

Rock grabbed Mia by the hair, hoisting her out of the chair. "You little bitch."

Logan heard a groan and a thud, but he didn't turn, praying Nick took out the idiot with the gun. Logan lunged forward just as Mia twisted her body, pushing the gun toward him, then smacking Rock in the eye with her fist.

Markus went for Rock, but Rock flung Mia like a sack of potatoes, hitting her brother with force and knocking them both to the floor.

Rock reached for Mia.

"I wouldn't do that if I were you," Logan said, scrambling to get the gun.

"Fuck you," Rock said, reaching down toward Mia, who scrunched under the desk.

"I've killed better men than you, so if you touch her again, I will shoot." Logan was done dealing with this prick.

"So will I," Nick said.

Logan shot one round, grazing Rock in the arm.

He groaned, grabbing his biceps as Nick breezed by Logan to secure Rock.

"Call your man off my mother."

"Already done." Markus hoisted himself up using the sides of the desk. His smile revealing a bloody mouth. "Trust me, your mother is fine."

Mia crawled out from the under the desk.

"Come here, baby," Logan dropped his weapon and scooped her into his arms. "Nick, get that piece of shit out of here before I strangle him." Sirens blared in the background. Logan put his earpiece back in. "Ramey? Dylan? Anyone got eyes on Mom?"

"I do and she's fine. Sniper in custody." Dylan's voice boomed into his right ear. "Your girlfriend has some skills. What she sees in a dumbass like you, I've got no clue."

Logan smiled as he held her tighter. "You okay, baby?"

"I am now." She let out a long breath, her arms wrapped tight around his middle.

"Mind telling me how you two knew my mother was fine?" Logan asked.

"As an incentive, Rock showed us the video, which gave Mia an idea." Markus wiped his face. "Can I go downstairs? I'm hungry."

Logan nodded. "What did you do, my brilliant little geek?" Logan kissed her temple, and her body trembled, or maybe it was his.

Her eyes brimmed with pride. "I hacked into my father's system and told him what happened. He told the police, and they were able to capture the sniper.

My dad then managed to let me know she was safe. We just kept the video going."

"That's smart." He kissed her forehead. "Is that what Rock flipped out over?"

She smiled bigger. "Not sure he even knows about that, but while he waited for you, I hacked into the video feed of the animal the world is waiting on to give birth. The world has been watching Rock confess to holding us against our will and using me to hack into the Department of Defense for the last ten minutes."

Logan cupped her face and stared into her loving eyes. "That was a dangerous little game."

"Your IT girl helped execute the plan. She would have stopped me if she thought it wouldn't have worked."

"But if my end of this op went south, then you and your brother would be dead."

"And what would you have done if you were me?"

"We could go on like this for another round of twenty questions," he said, licking his lips.

"Are you gonna kiss me or what?" she asked, smiling.

Logan growled as he pressed his lips hard on hers, shoving his tongue deep into her mouth. His pulse continued to beat faster than it should after the completion of an op, but the thought he could have lost her after he'd just found her made his body shiver. He pried his lips away, kissing her cheek and earlobe. "I love you," he whispered.

"I love you too."

Sirens blipped, and flashing lights filtered through the bedroom window. He heard an array of voices booming through the house.

"We need to go downstairs."

"Why?" She dropped her head to his shoulder. "I'd rather just curl up in your arms. It's been a long day."

He let out a small laugh. "One. We're going to spend the next few hours talking to all sorts of people. Two. I need to do something for your father."

Logan took her hand and led her down the hallway to the main staircase where half a dozen federal agents from various agencies were talking with twice as many Nightstalkers and Rangers than his brother Ramey had brought. Rock and all of his men were in restraints and being escorted outside by local and state police.

"Wait." Logan let go of her hand and jogged down the stairs, taking the last six two at a time. "I need a word with that one."

The officer holding Rock's arm stopped. "Fine with me."

Logan curled his fingers around Rock's arm. "Let's step outside."

Rock jerked his arm. "I'm not going anywhere with you."

Logan ignored Rock and hauled his ass outside where he eyed Mr. Vanderlin's car skidding to a stop just inside the gate.

*Perfect timing.*

Mr. Vanderlin stepped from his vehicle with wide, angry eyes.

Logan waved him over, then turned to Rock. "Years ago, my father arrested you for assaulting Mia, but unfortunately, all you got was a slap on the wrist."

"It was so much more than that," Rock said behind gritted teeth. "I had to change schools and the DA charged me, so that sucker stayed on my record. Why the fuck do you think I dropped out of college. That cunt—"

Logan shoved Rock to the ground, where he landed at Mr. Vanderlin's feet. "Say something like that again, and I'll beat the shit out of you. I'll even make it an almost fair fight by uncuffing you and letting you try to take a swing at me. But then, everyone would know what a goddamned pussy you are." Logan glanced at Mr. Vanderlin. "Sorry about the language, sir."

"Not a problem," Mr. Vanderlin said, his hands clenched at his sides. "Did he hurt my little girl again?"

Logan swallowed. "I wish I could tell you I was able to stop him before he yanked her by the hair."

"You bastard," Mr. Vanderlin said.

Logan hoisted Rock to his feet, who glanced between the two men with wide eyes. "I'm not bound by the same ethical and legal restraints my father was that night, so feel free."

Mr. Vanderlin raised his fist.

"What the fuck?" Rock tried to break free from Logan's grip. "You can't let him haul off and hit me."

Logan stepped back just as Mr. Vanderlin tossed his best punch, landing right on Rock's left eye. It might have been childish and slightly unprofessional to let Mr. Vanderlin take his potshot, but it sure did put a smile on the man's face.

Mr. Vanderlin then smacked the right side of Rock's jaw.

"You're going to regret this." Rock stumbled backward. "This isn't over."

"Have fun in prison," Logan said as a local cop

waltzed over, giving him the evil eye before ushering Rock away.

Mr. Vanderlin shook out his hand. "You have no idea how good that felt."

Logan smiled. "Felt good to watch."

"You're all right." Mr. Vanderlin slapped Logan on the back as they headed toward the house.

Mia leaned on the front porch, staring at him and smiling. How could a dumb jock like him end up with a woman like Mia Vanderlin?

"You're not so bad yourself, Mr. Vanderlin."

"You call me that or sir again, I'll give you my right hook."

"I'll remember that, sir...Mr.... I mean Brett." Logan shook his head. "It's going to take me a while to get used to that."

"I have feeling we have all the time in the world by the look you put on my daughter's face. All I ask is that you make her happy."

"I'll die trying."

# Chapter Fourteen

Two days later...

Logan slapped the water, splashing his brothers Nick and Ramey, before jumping on Dylan, giving him a good old-fashioned noogie. "We'll get them next time, baby Dyl."

"Don't call me that." Dylan shrugged his brother off before flipping himself onto a floaty. "I hate it," he muttered.

Logan climbed the ladder at the deep end of the pool, taking the towel Mia handed him. "Your parents didn't have to have all of us over."

"They wanted to. You and your family did a lot for us." She leaned up and kissed his cheek. "Want a beer?"

"I'd love one."

He twisted the towel in his hands, his fingers

itching to fling the fabric forward, smacking Mia on her adorable ass as she swayed her hips. She eyed him over her shoulder as she walked toward the outdoor bar, daring him to do it front of everyone.

Well, that wasn't going to happen. He winked at her, then sighed as he waltzed over to where his mother lounged, sipping some fruity drink.

"Hey, Mom." He bent over, giving his mother a kiss on the cheek before settling down in the chair next to hers.

"Thanks for bringing me all my boys, even if it's only for another eighteen hours."

"I needed their help."

"Ha!" His mother jabbed him in the arm with her index finger. "You have friends closer than Nevada. You asked Ramey to come not only to help you, but because you know how much I miss my boys."

Logan smiled. "I don't trust anyone as much as I do those clowns."

"Nick told me he's not going to re-enlist and has an interview with the Aegis Network."

"Tomorrow afternoon. I'll introduce him, then the rest is up to him."

His mother sighed. "I worry about him. Between

your father's death and Joann's, he's closed himself off from everything."

"The Aegis Network will be a good change of pace for him."

Mia appeared at his side, holding out a beer. "Thanks, baby." He spread his legs, resting his feet on the concrete, and patted the chair. She slid between his legs, leaning back on his chest. Seemed his life came full circle.

"I haven't had the chance to tell you how sorry I am that all this put you in danger," Mia said.

His mother waved her hand in the air. "I didn't even know I was in danger until after the fact. Really, the only negative is I have to find a new secretary. Can't believe I didn't recognize her as someone Dylan dated. I even contemplated fixing them up."

Logan shook his head, ignoring the statement. "If you really feel the need to continue to work, why don't you just run the agency? You could then take more time for yourself. Maybe take up golf?" Logan tried to give his mother his best rendition of his father's 'I'm right, listen to me' look, but by the way his mother laughed, it didn't work out too well. He tipped his beer and swigged.

"Tell you what." His mother patted his shoulder.

"I'll reduce my working hours if you knock this one up."

He coughed and gagged, and some of the beer drizzled out onto Mia's shoulder, who covered her face with both hands, shaking her head.

"Geez, Mom. I can't believe you said that out loud." Though he wasn't too shocked since his mother was all about babies.

His mother stood. "I'll let you two ponder that thought. But remember. I'll never be the mother of the bride, so the marriage thing?" She shrugged. "Not concerned with. But grandbabies? Little Sarich grandbabies? Yeah. I don't want to wait too long for those." With that statement, his mother turned and walked toward Mia's parents.

"Oh, God," Logan whispered, resting his hand on her taut stomach, her skin drenched with the hot sun. "She's going to talk babies with your parents."

Mia's middle tightened as she let out a soft laugh. "I think our mothers have started knitting little booties together."

"That's nuts." He fanned his thumb across her soft skin below her belly button, his mind wondering what it would be like to see her midsection swell with a new life.

"Not as crazy as us taking fourteen years to realize we loved each other."

"I suppose." He dropped his chin to her head. "We haven't talked about this, but any chance you can move to Orlando?"

"That can be arranged, but I have a few demands."

"Okay?" He swallowed.

"I'm not moving there to live alone, so I want to move in with you. I'm still going to work, but might change a few things about my career, but I don't expect you to give up the Aegis Network."

"All good with me." He kissed her temple.

"There's more."

"I'm listening." He took a sip of his beer. He'll agree to any and all of her demands as long as he got to spend the rest his life making hers better.

"The bootie thing? I don't want them to have to wait too long to actually make the booties. Maybe two years? Tops?"

He spewed his beer for the second time. Sure, his mind had wandered there, but he never expected her to voice it so...so...confidently.

"You don't like that idea?"

He cleared his throat. "No. I actually like it a lot. Totally on board with it... Did I just say that?" He tilted her chin to the side. "Mia Vanderlin, what have you done to me?"

She smiled, twisting her body until they were chest to chest.

"Our parents are watching," he whispered, trying not to glance to the other side of the pool and ignoring the heckles coming from his brothers.

"Considering they want us to give them grand-children, I don't think any one of them are going to have any problem with a little public display of affection."

He growled, wrapping his arms around her body. "Are you gonna kiss me, or what?"

---

Thank you for reading **THE LIGHTHOUSE**. I hope you will continue with the journey and pick up Nick's story: **HER LAST HOPE**. I've included an excerpt of his story. Also, I love hearing from readers, so please feel free to leave an HONEST review.

And I'd love for you to checkout the spin-off series: THE AEGIS NETWORK: THE EVERGLADES DIVISION

In a place where the past never stays buried and the

swamp keeps its own score, they're not just protecting the land—they're fighting to reclaim it.

Starting with the first two books:
*Hunted in Calusa Cove*
*Shadows in Calusa Cove*

*Sign up for my Newsletter (https://dl.bookfunnel. com/6atcf7g1be) where I often give away free books before publication.*

*Join my private Facebook group (https://www. facebook.com/groups/191706547909047/) where I post exclusive excerpts and discuss all things murder and love!*

Never miss a new release. Follow me on
Amazon:amazon.com/author/jentalty
And on Bookbub: bookbub.com/authors/jen-talty

# About Jen Talty

Jen Talty is the *USA Today* Bestselling Author of Contemporary Romance, Romantic Suspense, and Paranormal Romance. In the fall of 2020, her short story was selected and featured in a 1001 Dark Nights Anthology.

Regardless of the genre, her goal is to take you on a ride that will leave you floating under the sun with warmth in your heart. She writes stories about broken heroes and heroines who aren't necessarily looking for romance, but in the end, they find the kind of love books are written about :).

She first started writing while carting her kids to one hockey rink after the other, averaging 170 games per year between 3 kids in 2 countries and 5 states. Her first book, IN TWO WEEKS was originally published in 2007. In 2010 she helped form a publishing company (Cool Gus Publishing) with NY

*Times* Bestselling Author Bob Mayer where she ran the technical side of the business through 2016.

Jen is currently enjoying the next phase of her life... the empty nester! She and her husband reside in Jupiter, Florida.

Grab a glass of vino, kick back, relax, and let the romance roll in...

*Sign up for my Newsletter (https://dl.bookfunnel. com/82gm8b9k4y.) where I often give away free books before publication.*

*Join my private Facebook group (https://www. facebook.com/groups/191706547909047/) where I post exclusive excerpts and discuss all things murder and love!*

Never miss a new release. Follow me on Amazon: amazon.com/author/jentalty

And on Bookbub: bookbub.com/authors/jentalty

# Also by Jen Talty

*Brand New Series!*
*The Aegis Network: The Everglades*
*Division*
*Hunted in Calusa Cove*
*Shadows in Calusa Cove*

**Welcome to...Everglades Overwatch!**
*Secrets in Calusa Cove*
*Pirates in Calusa Cove*
*Murder in Calusa Cove*
*Betrayal in Calusa Cove*

*The Secrets of Stone Bridge*
*A Vintage of Regret*
*A Harvest of Lies*

***Whiskey Smash***
***Irish Whiskey***

***The Monroes***
***Color Me Yours***
***Color Me Smart***
***Color Me Free***
***Color Me Lucky***
***Color Me Ice***
***Color Me Home***

***Broken Heroes Mended Souls***
***Shelter for Danni***
***Shelter for Shay***

***Fallport Rescue Operations***
***Searching for Madison***
***Searching for Haven***
***Searching for Pandora***
***Searching for Stormi***
***Searching for Winslet***
***Searching for Odessa***

## DELTA FORCE-NEXT GENERATION
***Shielding Jolene***